(

"I'm leaving!" I s.... me. "I never want to see you again." I stormed throug... ... twilight of Civitavecchia in anger. My father and I have had a stormy relationship ever since my mother died. I suppose that every boy of 16 gets in fights with his father, but maybe I get in more fights than others. This fight started out like the others: "You've been out too late" or "you're neglecting your chores." Tonight was a new one, "You stole money from your mother!" "She's not my mother! My mother is dead." I shouted back. "She's nothing." I added, to drive in the hurt just a little more. My father's face clouded in fury as he shouted "She's your stepmother and deserves respect. She's done everything she can to give you a better life and this is how you pay back her kindness by stealing from her?"

To be honest I had stolen money from my stepmother. I had taken to meeting friends along the waterfront and needed some money. I didn't really regard it as stealing since she gets the money from my father and my father really should be giving me money.

I'll take a moment and introduce myself. My name is Leopold Fiori. Leopold means "bold man." My father sometimes says that he should have named me Antioco, which means "stubborn." We live in Civitavecchia, which is the port of Rome. Rome, of course, is the city of the Holy Father. The Pope. Civitavecchia is part of the Papal

States, the territory under the control of the pope. Right now in 1864 France has control of the city and port in order to protect the pope. I really don't get in to all the politics of who controls the city or Rome. I really don't care about the pope or church, but that's another fight my father and I have had.

There weren't always fights. When my mother was alive I remember smiles and laughter and my father bringing home fish for dinner from his job at the port. My mother would take the fish and prepare it with eggplant and serve it to us with a smile and a prayer of thanksgiving to St. Fermina, the patron saint of the city. Later she would tuck me in to bed with another prayer to the Virgin to keep me safe during the night.

But then things changed. My mother became ill. "Consumption," they called it. She coughed. She couldn't breathe and sometimes she coughed up blood. I would hurry home from school and sit by her side trying to tell jokes just to see a smile. It all came to an end one afternoon while I sat with her. She held my hand and whispered "such a good boy," and she was gone. I ran from the house, without thinking, and didn't stop till I was hunched over in dry heaves and tears somewhere along the waterfront.

"What's wrong?" came a voice from the shadows. I was so surprised to hear somebody that I didn't even think about looking like a crying little boy. "My mo…moth..mother." I stammered. "What happened boy?"

and now I could see it was a grizzled old man sitting on the side of the pier. Slowly and then in a gush of words I cried out everything that had happened and how I had tried to keep mother happy and now she was gone. He listened without words for a long time and when I had exhausted my own he finally said, "Yes. That's it. A good cry helps. It's going to feel bad but I promise it will get better." We sat there in silence for an hour with me crying softly and the old man not saying a word. Finally, sensing that I had cried myself out he said, "You go on now. Your family will be worried about you and you must be strong. If you need to talk old Giovanni will be here to listen. OK?" Suddenly feeling like a child, I turned and ran without saying a word of thanks.

I ran, but over the next several days I thought about Giovanni and his promise. The following week, after mother had been placed in the earth with the prayers of the faithful, I ventured back to the waterfront. "There you are boy," Giovanni shouted from the end of the pier where he was working, "come here and help me." I worked my way over to the end of the pier and helped him splice some rope. We worked in silence for awhile before I told him the events of the week. I talked for an hour about how I felt when I heard the sound of dirt being thrown on the grave and the loneliness I felt. Finally I looked up "I must go. See you soon." I was most of the way home before I realized that I hadn't told Giovanni my name and he hadn't said a word in the hour I was there.

The days turned in to weeks and weeks months as my grief turned to a hard ball in my heart. I would go to the pier once a week or so when my chores or school would allow it. A friendship developed between the boy and man as I poured out more and more of my heart to this man who listened more than spoke and only occasionally offered advice.

Ironically this friendship with Giovanni brought about other friendships that ultimately changed my life. One day as I was walking home from the pier I came upon boys from the town whom I only knew by sight. "Hey Leo," one of them shouted, using the diminutive of my name, "come here." A little surprised that they knew me, I went over. "Why are you here? This is our area. You don't come here unless we say so." I knew that they were testing me and I knew that it would be best to just walk away but something inside me would not let that happen. "Hey. I'll walk around here if I want," came the defiant reply. The big one shoved me and knocked me to the ground. I jumped up and the rage at my mother's death erupted in a series of blows against the face of the big one. This went on for a minute while the other boys stood there surprised that I had taken on the leader of the group. Finally they pulled me off him and held me on the ground. The big one laughed "Hey. You're pretty good with those fists. It's been a while since anybody's given me a bloody nose. You're all right!" He offered his hand and pulled me up from the ground. "I'm Fabiano and these two are Nardo and Vincenzo." I laughed to myself that the obvious leader of the group had a name that means "bean farmer" while the other two had names that had meant "strong" or "conquering." I didn't say anything but took the proffered hand. We moved away from the waterfront and sat in an alley and talked. Fabiano asked me what I had been doing. "I come sometimes and talk with Giovanni." I replied. "Old man Giovanni! You can do better than that. You stick with us and we will have fun." Nardo pulled a bottle from his jacket and offered us each a swig. The liquor burned going down my throat but I felt a kinship with boys my own age. Maybe they were right. Maybe Giovanni was just an old man. I walked home, happy that I had made some new friends, but conflicted that I had betrayed another.

FRIENDS AND CONSEQUENCES

My meetings with Giovanni came less and less as I spent more time with my new friends. I think he sensed that our relationship had changed as he sometimes questioned where I had been or why I didn't come around as often. Once he asked "Who were the boys I saw you with yesterday?" I hedged my reply by saying, "Oh, just some boys," and changed the subject. He didn't push the issue but I could tell he was hurt.

My father sensed that something was different too, but he was much more direct than Giovanni. "I don't know what you are doing while I'm at work, but you're not getting your chores done. Who are you with and what are you doing?" I snarled back "Nobody" and turned to stomp out of the house. "You stop right there." He shouted. "Things will be different now. I'm getting married to Lorenzo's daughter and you will treat her like your mother." I turned as if he had stabbed me in the heart. "No! She will never be my mother. How could you?" I stormed out of the house and didn't return that night.

I walked aimlessly along the waterfront until I realized that I was walking towards where I hoped to see Giovanni. Sure enough he was in his usual spot at the end of the pier. "There you are boy!" but he could tell I was upset and didn't say anymore, waiting for me to talk. "It's my father. He's getting married again." I said. Giovanni nodded. "Yes. That's not surprising. You know sometimes men just don't want to live alone. Maybe he got tired of being

alone." The rage that had been building inside me broke.
"No!" I shouted. "He shouldn't betray my mother. He
doesn't love her. I loved her." I could tell that I had hurt
him. I felt bad that I had shouted at him but didn't bother
to turn around and apologize and stormed back along the
pier.

I spent the night in the alley not too far from where I
had had the fight with Fabiano. It was cold, but I wasn't
going to give father the satisfaction of knowing he was
right. I wanted to hurt him more than I wanted to be warm.

The next day I didn't bother to go to school or look for
Giovanni. I was hungry but didn't want to go home to get
food. I debated about swallowing my pride and going
home or finding Giovanni and ask for food but just as I
was about to turn and go home I saw Nardo walking down
the street. "Hey Nardo," I shouted. "Come here." He saw
me and came over and then I saw Fabiano and Vincenzo
too. "I'm hungry. You have any food?" Fabiano laughed.
"Come. I'll show you how we do things." He turned and
led us down the street toward the market. "The market?" I
said. "I don't have any money to buy things at the market."
He looked at me like I was a child. "Money! We don't
need money. You go talk to the man selling bread. I turned
and saw him pointing at the baker. I went to the baker and
asked him how much a baguette cost but was shocked
when out of the corner of my eye I saw Fabiano reach out
and take a couple rolls of bread and shove them in his
pocket and walk away. I thanked the baker and walked

away. "Here," said Fabiano later as he handed me a roll. "You did good. The old man never suspected anything." I took the bread but it felt dry in my mouth; the taste of thievery.

I went home and my father wasn't there but returned later. He didn't say a word about me spending the night away from home but finally said, "I'm getting married next week. I want you to meet her." To my surprise I didn't leave the house or shout at my father. I just grunted "OK."

He brought her home that evening. "This is Maria, I will be marrying her. I miss your mother too but I can't live in the past." Maria turned out to be nice and greeted me with a kiss. "Oh Leopold. So good to meet you. I hope we can be friends." I was charmed by her beauty and kindness but then immediately felt guilty as if I was betraying my mother. I gave her a perfunctory kiss on the cheek and turned away. My father noticed my behavior but didn't say anything. Instead, looking at Maria, "Come my dear. Let's take a walk." And leaving me alone they walked out the door arm in arm. I looked after them as they left and felt anger. Anger at myself for acting as I had to what seemed like a nice woman and anger at my father for getting married again. I ran to my room and threw myself on my bad and cried myself to sleep.

The next few days passed without incident. Father reminded me, as if I had forgotten, that he was getting married. I muttered "yes I know," but didn't offer congratulations or ask if I could do anything. The day of the wedding dawned clear and father made me go with him to the church where we met Maria's family. Since it was the second marriage for both it was a simple ceremony. Maria's first husband had died at sea the previous year but she had no children from that marriage. At least that was one good thing, I thought darkly, I wouldn't have to share with anybody. The priest came and said a few words about the sanctity of marriage and the importance of raising children for the Church and pronounced them man and wife. I felt empty of emotion as I watched them leave the church arm in arm. We gathered at the home of Maria's parents for a dinner and her father toasted the new couple, "Long life and happiness to my daughter and new son!" Maria beamed in happiness and my father looked happier than I had seen him since mother died. I allowed a smile to go across my face. "Maybe it wouldn't be so bad to have a woman in the house." I thought. I promised myself that I would make it work.

The first few weeks things did go OK. I helped Maria but refused to call her "mother." She didn't seem to mind. One day I had been with the boys and came home late. It was the first time that I had really been out with the boys since the wedding. I got home and Maria asked "Where were you? Why are you so late?" I suppose she didn't sound too accusatory but I was tired and didn't feel like answering. "None of your business." I snapped, and immediately felt guilty, but didn't apologize. She smiled lightly "OK. Good night," and went to bed. She must have told my father because the next day he scolded me "Maria is your mother now. You must treat her with respect." I nodded but didn't apologize to Maria or my father.

I spent more time out of the house with Fabiano, Nardo, and Vencinzo. Together we roamed the city sometimes stealing some bread or fruit from the market. They still used me as bait to talk to the shop owner while the others stole something. I suppose I should have felt guilt over this but I was having too much fun being with friends my own age and acting a man. I hadn't seen Giovanni since the night I had yelled at him and I felt guilty about that too. I vowed that I would return to the pier and search for him.

I vowed but I never made it. One afternoon we were out and, as usual, none of us had money. Fabiano pointed out a house. "That's where old Amici lives. He's rich. We can sneak in to the house and grab some money and not worry about a thing for weeks." I felt uneasy about this. Taking some fruit or bread from the market was one thing, but this was stealing plain and simple. I had told myself that taking money from Maria was OK because it was really money from my father that he owed me. This would be hard to justify. "Here Leo. You're the smallest. We'll push you up through the window and then you can pull me up and the two of us can hoist up Nardo," said Fabiano. I thought about walking away from the group but after all the petty thefts we had done I supposed it was too late.

The three of them stood by a back window and carefully pushed me up the side of the house. From there I was able to pull myself into the house and hold out my hands for Fabiano who stood on Nardo's shoulders to reach the window. We entered a quiet house and searched through a couple of rooms finding nothing of value. "Shit," said Fabiano. "They have nothing." Finally in the third room we found a desk with drawers. We opened the drawer and found money. Not a lot of money but enough to keep us in snacks or tobacco for a week. Fabiano grabbed the money and shoved it in his pocket. "OK. Let's go," was the command. We crept back to the back window and reversed the procedure the way we entered. I was the last person out the window and as I was lowering myself out the window with my feet on Nardo and Vincenzo's shoulders a woman walked into the room we had just exited. "Thief!" She shouted. "Stop thief!" The boys heard and ran leaving me hanging by the window and then falling to the ground. The woman ran to the window. "I see you!" She shouted at me and the backs of the other boys. I took off running behind the other boys afraid that somebody would catch me and turn me back to my father. I ran to catch up with the boys but couldn't find them. Finally it dawned on me. There was no honor among thieves. As soon as they heard the woman shouting they had fled. Fabiano had the money and the only one who had been seen was me. I wondered if he had planned it that way.

I walked home, dejected. I had made a fool of myself.

I walked in the house to see my father with rage in his eyes. "You stole from your mother!" He shouted. He was right. I had stolen from Maria and then I had helped to steal from the Amici's. He was right, but I couldn't admit it. Cornered, I couldn't admit that he was right and I couldn't tell him how I had just disgraced myself. Rage and shame boiled up. Rage at the death of my mother that I had never been able to understand. Shame at how I had been played for a fool by my "friends." I regretted the words as they came out of my mouth, but was unable to stop the flow, "I'm leaving! I never want to see you again!"

THE NOVARA

I found myself walking along the pier. I had made a wreck of my life. I had destroyed any relationship with my father and Maria. If the lady from the Amici household did recognize me she wouldn't waste any time talking to my father, or worse yet, the police. I needed to talk to somebody. Then I remembered. Giovanni. Yes. I would talk to him. He never got mad at me and always listened to me. I would look for him. I walked along the pier where he usually worked but didn't see him. I walked the length of the pier looking for him. I only saw one ship decked out in flags and banners. I avoided the ship and continued further up the waterfront. Finally I could wait no more. I approached a man and asked if he knew where Giovanni was. "Giovanni?" He replied. "Old man Giovanni? He's dead. Died yesterday." The bottom dropped out of my world. "You know him? You a relative?" His questions followed me down the street. I really had destroyed everything now and even the one man I thought could help me was gone. I continued back along the waterfront and in the distance I heard somebody "That looks like the kid that stole from the Amici house. Grab him and see if she can recognize him." I didn't wait for anybody to come after me and without thinking I took off running down the pier as fast as I could. I got to the end and realized I was stuck. The only thing in front of me was the ship I had seen earlier. It was covered in banners and flags that I didn't recognize. I studied the ship for a few minutes behind boxes that looked like they were ready to be loaded. I did recognize the Austrian eagle on one flag but not the eagle on the other green and red flag. There was a guard at the gangplank who looked like he was half asleep but I didn't see anybody above deck. I could see now she was named "Novara." At the other end of the pier I could see several men heading my way. One looked like a policeman. I looked at the ship and looked again down the pier. I made the decision that would change my life. I ran and jumped grabbing for a rope that hung from the side of the ship.

I hung from the side of the ship. The guard hadn't heard and still stood at his post looking bored. I was lucky in that I had been able to hide behind the boxes till the last second. Any sound that I had made by hitting the side of the ship was muffled by the sound of birds and waves. I hung for a minute and then hand over hand pulled myself on deck. I hid on deck behind more boxes that looked like they had just come on board. On the pier I heard rather than saw several men walk up the pier. "You there! Sailor! Have you seen a boy come by here?" Even though I couldn't see him, I could hear his voice and it almost seemed to stand at attention. "No sir. Nobody has come by here."

I was relieved. I heard steps go down the pier and thought if I waited I could get off the ship and go home to repair the relationship with my family. I was just about ready when I heard steps coming along the deck. I heard voices but they were speaking what sounded like German.

They were coming closer and closer. I looked around for an escape route but saw nothing except an open door to an inner cabin. At the last possible second I dove for the open door and found myself in an ornate cabin. I was going to wait here for the German speakers to leave and then go out on deck again. As if the fates were conspiring against me I heard them come toward the door. I searched again for a place to hide and saw another door that led to stairs going down in to the depths of the ship. Without thinking I jumped through the door and down the stairs. By this time I felt like a trapped rat and searched for anyplace I might hide. I ran through doors and stairs as quietly as I could till I finally reached the ship's hold. In the dim light I could only see a passageway down the middle of the hold and I took off running as fast as I could at the sound of voices behind me. Too late I saw the beam across the deck above me. I heard, rather than felt the pain as my head exploded against the beam and I collapsed.

THE STOWAWAY

I don't know how long I was out. When I woke I had a splitting headache. I tried to move and the pain only increased. Something felt different about the ship. It felt like we were moving. I tried moving again and the pain increased tenfold, and I went unconscious again.

I woke to somebody throwing water on my face, "How long has he been here? Did anybody see him come aboard? We must inform His Majesty." The man, whoever he was, pulled me roughly to my feet. My head exploded in pain again and I vomited all over him and went unconscious again. This time I wasn't lucky enough to stay unconscious but woke nearly immediately as the man swore and pulled me roughly up the steps. "Here." He shouted at a soldier. "You allowed somebody to come aboard. Bind him till we determine what the Emperor would like to do with him." He stormed away with my vomit dripping from his clothes. I knew this wasn't going to end well.

The soldier worked quickly and soon I was bound hands behind my back and legs tied together. "Emperor!" I thought. "What have I gotten myself in to?" Soon another man came and introduced himself, "I'm Felix Eloin, advisor to his Imperial Majesty Maximilian. How did you get onboard?" I recounted briefly how I jumped at the rope leaving out how I was hiding from the police. "Please sir. May I just go ashore and go home? I didn't mean anything. My family will be worried by now." "Go ashore!" He laughed. We've been at sea two days now on our way to

Mexico, and you, boy, are a stowaway. The Emperor will decide what is to be done with you."

My head swam in pain as I realized what I had done. I had been unconscious for two days and in that time we had set sail for someplace called Mexico. I had never even heard of this place before and wondered how far it was from home. Who was this Emperor Maximilian? I had heard of Napoleon of course, and even Franz Josef, the Austrian Emperor, but never one called Maximilian. Eloin continued, "What's your name, boy? We might as well get that taken care of before we take you to the Emperor." "Leopold," I said. "Well, that will make Her Majesty happy at least," Eloin continued with what I hoped was a joke. "maybe they won't throw you overboard."

I was left alone tied to a post with a gag in my mouth. Soon two soldiers came, and keeping my arms tied behind my back, untied me from the post and pulled the gag from my mouth. I was brought up the steps to the first cabin that I had entered, what seemed, an eternity ago.

Sitting at the far end of the room was a couple, who, I could only assume were the Emperor and Empress. Of where or what I didn't know. As we approached the couple the soldiers roughly pushed my head and shoulders down in a bow, while one growled "Bow before the Emperor, boy." I managed to complete the bow and knew enough to say, "Your Majesty." The Emperor, tall and blond with a beard that couldn't hide a small chin, looked at me and said, "Well boy. The captain tells me that you are a stowaway. What is your story? Or shall we do away with niceties and throw you overboard?" He added with a chuckle. The Empress, a petite woman with dark hair, answered "Oh Your Majesty. Can't you see he's afraid? What's your name my boy?" Remembering that Eloin had said that would make her happy I said, "My name is Leopold, Your Majesty." She beamed with happiness. "There you go my dear. You must be good to this boy for he carries the name of my father." The Emperor laughed with her. "Now, Leopold, tell us your story." At this point I decided that the whole truth would be better so I started with how I had helped steal the money from the Amici's only to be left to be caught alone. I continued with getting into the fight with my father over stealing money from Maria. Finally I concluded with how I had discovered that Giovanni had died and was trying to escape from police to get back home when I had come aboard the ship. I purposely did not use the word "stowaway." "Please Sir. Can you take me home? The last thing I said to my father was 'I don't want to see you again.' I want to make things right." The Empress looked sad while the Emperor paused for a moment. "Well my boy. That will be difficult. Already we are two days at sea while you were unconscious. I'm afraid that you are with us on our journey to Mexico." I listened to him with little understanding. "Please Sir. Where is Mexico? Maybe I can walk from there to Rome." With that even the soldiers laughed. "My boy," said Maximilian, "Mexico is far from here. Several weeks by ship to the Americas." For the second time in hours my world fell apart.

THE EMPEROR AND EMPRESS

I was removed from the presence of the royal couple and I struggled to keep from crying. I was returned to the room where I was originally tied hand and feet. "Well," asked a soldier. "do we untie the boy?" The second soldier replied, "The Emperor didn't say what to do with him. He only said that he was with us now on our way to Mexico. God help us all. Leave him tied here till we're told what to do." Since my arms had never been untied from behind my back I was tied again by my feet with the gag stuffed roughly in my mouth. They shoved me in a chair and left. I sat there, glad now for the gag in my mouth, since it muffled my cries. I sat there with my head on my chest and tears running down my face. "How could you be so stupid?" I thought. Father was right. My name shouldn't be "Leopold," bold man. It should be "Antioco," for I truly was stubborn. My stubbornness had gotten me this far. I was stubborn when dealing with my father and stubborn when Giovanni tried to calm me. I should have walked away from a fight the first time I met Fabiano and the others, but even then I stubbornly refused to think logically and followed them into what became larger and larger crimes of theft.

I think I sat there in tears for an hour and eventually I felt the presence of somebody in the room. I thought it was another soldier and I tried to wipe my tears on my shoulder so that he wouldn't see me crying. Instead I heard a soft woman's voice. "Leopold. Are you all right? The Empress asked me to come and check on you." I rubbed my eyes even harder against my shoulders, hoping that my tears were dry. "Yes." I mumbled through the gag. Then realizing that I hadn't eaten since before we had robbed the Amici house. "Please M'am. Is there any food? I'm hungry. I haven't eaten for two days." Of course with the gag in my mouth it didn't sound like that but she understood. The woman laughed. "I think we can find you some food. We can't have a death onboard the Emperor's ship, now can we?" She turned and called for a soldier. "I think we can untie the boy. The Empress Charlotte is concerned about him." This time the soldier was gentle as he untied me and pulled the gag from my mouth.

"Come, Leopold," said the woman. "We will find you some food in the galley," and she led me down a corridor. I quickly discovered that a galley was a kitchen. I suppose I should have known that but I had never worked on a ship before, but only around them on the pier. "Cook. Can we give some food to Leopold? He shall be with us for the duration." "Yes M'am," said the cook. "He looks like he could use something. Can you work boy?" Then, without waiting for a reply, "Good. We will need all the help we can to get to Mexico and God's help once we get there. Begging your pardon, M'am." This was twice that somebody had implied that troubles awaited in Mexico. I wondered why people were worried. "Don't worry him now Cook. Let's just feed him," said the woman. "Yes M'am," came the quick reply. The woman brought me to a small table in a room adjoining the galley. "Come. Let's sit here and talk. I think you must have many questions. I am Countess Kollonitz, lady in waiting to Her Majesty the Empress Charlotte. You may call me "Countess." She concluded firmly. "Yes M'am… er Countess. Please M'am. Countess. Why are we going to Mexico and who are the Emperor and Empress? I've only heard of Napoleon of France and Franz Josef of Austria. Are there others?" She smiled at my questions. "Well, It looks like we will have a long story to tell you. Here comes some food so go ahead and eat and I'll tell you what is happening."

She proceeded to tell me the story of Maximilian and Charlotte. Maximilian's brother is the Emperor Franz Josef of Austria. That would explain why I saw the Imperial flag on the ship the night I jumped onboard. He is married to Charlotte whose father is Leopold, King of the Belgians. Maximilian is on his way to become Emperor of Mexico, as requested by the Mexicans, with the backing of France. That would explain the other flag that I saw on the ship, the flag of Mexico. "But Countess, M'am. Why was the ship in Civitavecchia? That's a long way from France or Austria?" The Countess replied patiently, "Why to get the blessings of the Pope of course. The Holy Father must give his blessing to this undertaking so that the Gospel can spread across the Americas." She continued, "The Holy Father personally said a Mass for the Emperor and Empress before they left Rome. Then of course there was the big send off at the ship with the gun salute and Ambassadors of France and Austria saying farewell. Certainly you heard that?" I confessed that I hadn't heard a thing. "This must have all happened after I came on board the ship and knocked myself unconscious." I rubbed my head as I spoke and the memory of it gave me a headache. "Well, when we get to Mexico you will see a welcome to exceed the farewell in Europe. The votes are in from the states and it is a mandate for the Empire!" Then, finally noticing me rubbing my head, "Oh, you poor boy. I'll have the doctor check on you. In the meantime make sure you get enough to eat." With that the Countess gave my cheek a touch and turned to leave. "I shall tell the Empress that you are well, but the doctor shall have the final say. Perhaps Her Majesty will call for you." With that she turned and left the room.

The cook, hearing her leave the room, entered and said, "Mark my words, boy. This will not end well. We are sailing in to trouble." I sat there, dumbfounded while he continued, "The Mexicans don't want an outside Emperor to come in and 'save' them. It's a battle weary country now, but it's not going to get any better with the arrival of more French soldiers." I tried to take this all in. "But sir." I started. "Don't call me sir. I work! Call me Georg. I've been a cook for the Austrian Navy since I was your age. I'll go where the Navy sends me but I won't keep my mouth shut. The French army is in for trouble when they land in that hole. Yes. I'll be glad to lift anchor and leave

Vera Cruz when we drop off the Emperor and his wife. The Archduke is a good man. I think he's been drawn into a quagmire." I interrupted again, "But Georg, who is the Archduke and why are French soldiers going to Mexico?" Georg laughed, "The Archduke? "That's Maximilian. His title is Archduke of Austria. Well he was Archduke till his brother the Emperor had him sign away his rights in Austria to become Emperor of Mexico. No, he is very popular in Austria and Venice." Looking both ways as if to make sure nobody was listening, he continued, "If you ask me, and I'll tell you if you don't ask. Franz Josef was more than willing to send the Archduke off to Mexico to keep him half a world away from the throne of Austria." He paused, and checked around again, "As far as why are there French soldiers here. Money! That's why! Napoleon is searching for money and power. Think about it boy! Why do wars start? Money and power!" I thought for a minute. I didn't know too much about wars, but I did know that France controlled my city. "Is that why the French are in Civit…" I started. "Of course that's why they are in Civitavecchia! Money and power." He calmed down for a minute and continued, "Mexico owes money to Europe so Napoleon is sending in a European to try and collect the money and spread his influence. Fortunately for Napoleon the United States is at war with itself so they don't have time or inclination to get involved in Mexico. Mark my words boy, if the North wins the war in the United States the president will call for an attack on a European king in Mexico!"

I was about ready to ask Georg to tell me more about Mexico and Austria, but at that moment the doctor arrived. "Well, my boy. You must have made an impression! The Empress herself asked me to come check on you. I understand you knocked yourself out coming aboard ship." With that he checked my eyes and felt the top of my head. "Yes, you have a bump all right. Your skin isn't clammy. Georg put some hot water bottles on his feet and he'll be good as new." I didn't know how hot water bottles on my feet would help my head but I wasn't going to argue with the doctor. The doctor left and Georg spent some time looking for some kind of water bottle he could use for my feet. "Sounds stupid to me," he muttered. "Should have put something cold on your head. Oh well. What do I know? I'm just a cook. The doctors make all the money." He found a bottle and filled it with hot water, "There you go boy. Direct from Doctor Georg of the Austrian Navy. Long live the Emperor!" I smiled and laughed with him in spite of the pain from my head. He talked more than Giovanni ever did but I think he really did care for me.

We were in the middle of a laugh when Eloin walked in. "It looks like you're not in too much pain. The Emperor has called for you. Be on your best behavior and show proper respect." He glanced at Georg as if he knew Georg's thoughts about the Mexican Empire or Franz Josef of Austria.

I worked my way back up to the cabin where I had been earlier. It was empty but a sailor pointed me to another cabin. "There is His Majesty's office. Knock first and make sure to bow. Don't waste his time. He is a busy man." I could tell that this sailor was Austrian for he spoke with pride of Maximilian. I could see why Georg said that he was very popular at home and I could understand why Franz Josef would be insecure. I knocked quietly on the door and tried to keep my knees from shaking. From inside came a curt, "enter" and I opened the door. Maximilian sat at a desk piled with papers. He looked tired but smiled when he saw me. "Well Leopold. Her Majesty and the Countess both tell me that they believe your story and we can trust you. Her Majesty, of course, trusts your name as it is the name of her father the king. I tried to keep my face noncommittal, "Yes Your Majesty. It was the name of my grandfather but sometimes my father says he should have named me "Antioco." Maximilian laughed before I could explain the meaning and said, "Ha. So you are stubborn eh? Well. There are worse things in life." I felt relaxed enough to laugh now and look up. Again I realized how blond he was and now that he was laughing I noticed his bad teeth and how they made his mouth look ugly. I immediately felt guilty for thinking that way and lowered my head. The Emperor took that as modesty and continued. "Since you will be with us now it is only right that you earn your keep. What can you do onboard the ship?" I thought for a minute. I didn't know anything about sailing to say I could help. I also didn't know anybody onboard except for Georg. "Please Sir. Your Majesty. May I help Georg in the galley? I would like to learn how to cook. "Done," said Maximilian. I'll tell Schertzenlechner that you are to help in the galley. Her Majesty and the Countess will be happy if you can learn to prepare delicious meals." He called out "Schertzenlechner", and in entered a man. "This is my private secretary Sebastian Schertzenlechner. He is in charge of the staff." Continuing,"Take this boy down to the galley and tell the cook he has a new helper. Then tell the Countess Kollonitz the same thing. Oh I suppose you better tell Eloin since he's the one who found him. Maybe the boy can make up for vomiting all over him." With a wink at me I was dismissed and I followed Schertzenlechner down to the galley again. "Well boy, is it true that you vomited all over Eloin?" He questioned. I got the feeling that he would be very happy that I had and that there was no love lost between the two. Trying to be as diplomatic as possible I said, "Unfortunately it is true that I was sick today." Schertzenlechner chuckled and muttered under his breath, "Good man!" I determined to ask Georg what was going on between the two.

When we arrived in the galley Schertzenlechner rather haughtily said, "It is His Majesty's command that this boy help in the galley. Any questions to His Majesty should be delivered through me." Georg smiled and said, "Yes sir. Thank you. I will put him to good work. Please thank His

Majesty for thinking of me!" Schertzenlechner turned to leave and Georg put his fingers to his lips while the private secretary left the galley. "Old buffoon! Thinking I would have questions about getting more help around here! Come boy! Let's get busy with supper!"

I discovered that I worked well with Georg even though I had never set foot in a kitchen, or galley, before. He was patient enough with me when I admitted that I didn't know anything about cooking. "Well, you'll just learn, won't you?" was his reply. He quickly showed me around the galley and pointed out some of his utensils. "There lad, remember that," he said more than once. "Here!" he said, handing me a knife. "What?" I replied taking the knife. "Start peeling." He commanded. And so my first job in a galley/kitchen was to peel potatoes. When I had completed a small bucket he glanced at my work. "It looks like you did leave some potato in the bucket. I guess you'll learn."

We were still preparing dinner when the Countess appeared at the door, "Her Majesty would like dinner served in her cabin. She will be working there." Georg looked up with a smile, "Yes M'am. I'll send up the boy with dinner shortly." With a quick, "Thank you," she disappeared. "Here lad." Georg gestured to a cabinet. "Make yourself look presentable so Her Majesty won't throw you overboard. Find a shirt so you won't go before royalty wearing potato peelings."

A few minutes later after finding something I could wear and putting together a tray of food I left the galley and ventured above deck in search of the Royal cabin. After several wrong turns I was directed to a cabin on the main deck. I stopped at the door and was about to knock when I suddenly thought, "I'm standing at the door of an Empress. What do I do? What if I do something wrong?" I stood there stupidly for a moment and realized that I needed to knock on the door but was holding the dinner tray with both hands. My first thought was to put the tray on the deck so that I could knock the door but somehow that didn't seem right to put food meant for royalty on the floor. I started to shift the tray to one hand so that I could knock with the other but in my nervousness my hand started to shake and the tray flew out of my hand. With a crash the tray and dinner landed on the deck. Broken pottery mixed with boiled potatoes and meat and gravy spread across the deck. In a flash I was on my knees trying to clean up the mess before anybody noticed. If I was lucky I could clean up everything and return to the galley to confess to Georg and start over again. Unfortunately, that was not to be. I was kneeling directly in front of the cabin door when I heard steps and the door opened and above my head appeared Her Royal Majesty Empress Charlotte of Mexico. "I'm sorry Your Majesty," and suddenly stuttering, "The t..ttt.tt ray f,ff,f ell out of my h.hhh.h.hand." I could tell she was looking at me and the mess but I didn't dare raise my face to look her in the eyes. Finally she said with a smile. "Thank you, but I prefer eating in my cabin and not out on deck. Why don't you clean up this mess and tell the cook that there was an accident." With that she closed the door and left me with broken crockery.

I returned to the galley and confessed to Georg. He laughed, but said, "You have to be careful boy, but most of all you have to learn to have confidence in yourself and be a strong man. This wouldn't have happened if you hadn't been so worried about appearing before Her Majesty would it?" I realized he was right. Perhaps if I had been more of a man I wouldn't have found myself a stowaway on board a ship bound for Mexico. The realization rocked me for a moment but I was pushed out of my reverie by Georg saying, "OK. Get a new tray set out and try it again. Practice now holding a tray with one hand." I returned to the Imperial cabin and with a new found grace I was able to knock on the door. "Enter," came the voice of the Empress. I opened the door and found her sitting at her desk in front of a pile of papers. "Place the food there," she said, pointing to a side table. "Leopold isn't it? My face flushed that she remembered my name until I remembered that I shared the name of her father. "Yes M'a…. Your Royal Highness," then added, "I hope to do justice to the name." She laughed. "I'm sure you will. His Majesty tells me that you have been assigned to the cook. Do you like it?" Feeling suddenly at ease I said, "Yes M'am, Your Majesty. Georg is very nice to me and I think I'll learn a lot." Then in what I thought was a joke I continued. "I've learned to peel potatoes!" Suddenly wishing I could call back my words I stood there stupidly. "Well. Thank you Leopold. You may go back to the galley now. In the future when you address me or His Majesty you say 'Your Majesty' the first time and then 'M'am' or 'Sir' later. Understand?" Embarrassed I said "Yes M'am. Thank you M'am." I started to turn to leave, and thinking better of it I backed to the door and left.

I returned to the galley and told Georg what had happened. "Yes. You should only speak when spoken to when you're around royalty. But you were right to not turn your back on the Empress. It would not be polite. Now change back in to your work clothes and we will clean the galley."

While we were working I asked how he knew so much about the Emperor. "I have spent thirty years at sea cooking in all types of ships. Ferdinand Maximilian is most happy when he is at sea. I was cook when he made his first tour of Venice in 1845. He was young then. Maybe younger than you, thirteen or fourteen. He was sent with his brothers Ludwig and the Prince, now Emperor, Franz Josef. I remember when they arrived he was so excited. There were throngs of people along the waterfront and he was told that they were all there just for him and his brothers. Now you have to know that the Italians do not want to be ruled by the Hapsburgs." I interrupted, "Who are the Hapsburgs?" Georg continued, "Hapsburg is the family name for the royal family of Austria. The kingdom of Venice was handed over to Austria by Napoleon after

France lost to Austria." He continued from where I had interrupted, "Now you have to know that the Italians hate the Hapsburgs. Those boys were told that the crowds of people were there to cheer for them and the Empire. What a joke. The people of Venice were out to see the new gas lighting of the city." I chuckled at the idea of somebody playing such a big trick on a prince. I questioned, "So has he spent his entire life at sea?" "Not all the time, my boy," came the reply. "I'm sure he would like it, but he's second son and was second in line to the throne. He's also very popular with the people so I'm sure the Emperor is very glad to have him far from Vienna." I was curious, "So where has he been if the Emperor wants him away from Vienna?" Georg laughed. "He was very popular as admiral of the Austrian Navy, and then he was governor of Venice. I understand that, while the people hated the Hapsburgs and the Empire, they personally liked Maximilian. He stayed there till his brother called him back to Vienna. Since then he's been pushed to the sidelines and has stayed at his palace at Miramar." "Miramar? Where's that?" I questioned. "It's the castle that he built for himself on the Adriatic Sea near Trieste. That's where we came from before Rome. Oh those were exciting days." He paused as if trying to remember everything. "What happened?" I asked. "Oh so much was going on. We were supposed to leave several days earlier but something happened. There were rumors that Maximilian was sick, but I don't know. Anyway, when we finally left there were banners flying and all the servants were crying. Nobody in Miramar or Trieste wanted to see Maximilian and Charlotte leave. Maximilian came on board and went right to his cabin. He didn't leave till you were presented to him in the main cabin. Schertzenlechner brought his meals to him or had me bring them up. If you ask me I think he's conflicted about going to Mexico. But what do I know? I'm just a simple cook." I started to ask another question but he cut me off. "Enough questions for now. We have work to do and I don't know why he picked Mexico. You need to learn in this life that God gave you two ears and only one mouth. You have to listen twice as much as you talk. If you want to learn about Mexico and Maximilian you have to pay attention to what's going on."

THE VOYAGE

Life quickly gained a routine as we made the six week voyage across the ocean. I threw a mat down on the floor in the small cabin next to the galley where the Countess had given me a meal and that is where I slept. Since I was called a stowaway and came with no baggage I had to beg for clothes and blankets for my bedroll. The first few days at sea I was pretty cold at night, but later as we worked our way south it warmed up. Georg and I spent the day cooking and I was often sent to deliver lunch or dinner to the Imperial couple. Her Majesty, the Empress Charlotte, or, as she liked to be called now, Carlota, using the Mexican version of her name, usually ate alone at her desk. Sometimes she joined the Emperor for meals. I usually came prepared with two meals just in case they were eating together. If she were alone she might have me leave the extra meal or have me deliver it to him in his cabin. I now had it down to a science. I would stand at the door and knock with one hand, while holding the tray with the other hand. She or the Emperor would call out "Enter," and I would enter with a short bow saying, "Your Majesty," and place the meal on a side table. From there I would quietly set the table and wait to be dismissed. Usually she would just say, "Thank you Leopold, you are dismissed," and with a "Yes M'am," I would leave.

One day I knocked on the door and instead of the Empress calling out it was Schertzenlechner who opened the door. He looked at me "Bring a meal for their

Majesties and myself. We shall be working here," and shut the door in my face.

I stood there surprised for a moment and was just ready to turn and go back to the galley for more food when I heard murmurs from the cabin change to sounds of heavy discussion. "What he did was nothing less than blackmail!" I heard the Empress say. Schertzenlechner agreed with "Yes, Your Majesty. The Empress is correct. The Emperor called it 'The Family Pact' but it was really his way to remove you from the family. You must renounce it." I wanted to stay and hear more but I didn't dare look too obvious. I left the cabin door, determined to ask Georg what he made of it.

While we quickly prepared trays for three I told Georg what I had heard. "Yes. That's what I mentioned once. Franz Josef had the Archduke sign away his rights as part of the Hapsburg family. It really meant that he had no right of succession in case anything happened to Franz Josef but it also took away his royal allowance. He called it 'The Family Pact.' I wonder what they are up to. Oh well. Makes no difference to us swabbies. Take the food up to them and be quick about it," came the command.

I went as quickly as I could carrying three meals when I arrived I paused for a moment before knocking, perhaps hoping I could hear something. I wasn't disappointed. From within I clearly heard Charlotte/Carlota saying, "Father's telegram said 'Max must give up nothing.'" Then, from the Emperor, "We are agreed? We shall say that we never saw the 'Act of Renunciation' until it was forced upon me before we left?" I heard some murmurs of assent and chose that as my time to knock at the door. This time the Emperor shouted "Enter," and I came in with the three meals. There was a silence while I set the table and without a word from them I recognized it as my time to leave. With a quick bow and "Your Majesties," I left the cabin. I paused for a minute in hopes that I would hear something else, but the cabin remained silent. With a shrug of my shoulders I returned to the galley.

I wanted to act more like a man and not gossip what I had heard but I had to ask Georg what it meant. I knew he would be honest. "Well boy. The first thing is that if you hear something you should keep it to yourself. Especially if it involves the Royal Family. If you say something and it gets around you will be in more trouble than being a stowaway aboard a Royal ship." He continued, "In this case I don't think it's any secret among Austrians or the upper class that he was forced to sign the 'Family Pact,' and now it sounds like they are planning to release another document saying they were forced to sign." I questioned, "What does that mean about Mexico?" With a laugh he replied, "Mean? They are stuck with no escape! They should never have agreed to go to Mexico but both have such high ideals of 'duty' and 'divine right' that they would never back down." Confused I asked "What is divine right?" "Divine Right! The belief that God has set kings above us common folk to rule us. That is why you must always bow your head and never turn your back on the Emperor. That is why you must always say, 'Your Majesty' when entering a room. They believe they have a mandate from God to reign. Now Europe thinks they can plant an empire on the steps of the United States. No. There were songs in Rome before we left 'Don't leave Max. The hangman awaits.' No. There is nothing good for them in Mexico." I started to ask another question but he cut me off. "No. You must be careful of what you say to other people. That's a good idea for life, and especially when dealing with royalty. Try to figure things out by yourself."

I went to bed that night in the next room and I lay awake for a long time thinking about my life. I had not thought about my words before I said them in my past. Certainly not with my father. I hadn't thought about my actions either. I suppose if I had I would have been sleeping in my own bed and going to school. I wondered if my father and Maria missed me. I wondered if he had asked police if they had seen me or if the Amici family connected a missing boy to a robbery. No, I had certainly messed up my life so far. Tears came unbidden to my eyes and I said, "God, can you fix this?" I fell asleep only to dream about Maximilian climbing a hill and a crowd singing in the background "Don't leave Max. The Hangman awaits the divine right." Charlotte was standing in a fountain crying "Bring me a chicken, Bring me a chicken….." I woke myself screaming "Bring me a chicken. Bring me a chicken," and I felt relieved it was just a dream and glad that nobody could hear me.

I slept so poorly that I was glad Georg kept me busy the next day running errands around the ship. It was really the first time that I had been allowed to explore the Novara and she was larger than I thought with six decks. After exploring her I wasn't surprised that it took them two days to find me passed out in the hold. She was about fourteen years old, having been launched in 1850. I wondered why ships were always called she. I thought about asking Georg but decided I would wait and see if I could find the answer by listening to what other people had to say.

We had been on the way several weeks and I was starting to feel at home on the ship. Georg asked me if I was going to return to Europe on the ship after we dropped the Imperial Couple off in Mexico. I was shocked. I hadn't even thought about getting home, I had been so busy just learning this new life. "You had better ask the captain if you can return with us. He might be willing to take on another deckhand." I hadn't seen the captain since the day I was pulled out of the hold. I imagine he was angry that someone had gotten past his security, but I hoped he wouldn't hold that against me. I asked the best way to meet the captain. "Go up and ask one of the officers if you can talk to the captain. That will be the best." After delivering lunch I gathered up courage to talk to the captain. I went up to a sailor and said, "Sir. I would like to talk to the captain. Could you help me?" He looked at me in fury. "You want to talk to the captain! I have half a mind to throw you overboard like we should have done that first day. I was docked a week's pay because I didn't see you come onboard." With that he backhanded me so hard against the side of my head that I fell to the deck. Once on the deck he looked at me and with a vicious kick growled, "Pray to God I don't see you before Vera Cruz or I'll toss you overboard myself." I lay on deck in pain and wondered if anybody saw. I looked around and the only sailors I saw were talking amongst themselves with an occasional glance in my direction. I'm pretty sure they saw the whole thing but weren't going to interfere. If I cost one sailor a week's pay I'm sure I wasn't too popular with the other sailors.

Nevertheless I wasn't going to let that stop me and I vowed to try again to talk to the captain. The next day gave me another opportunity. I was returning from bringing dinner to the Emperor and I saw the Head Steward and decided he was my best chance to talk to the captain, "Please Sir. I would like to talk to the Captain. Could you help me?" He looked at me, and for a moment I thought he was going to say no, but finally he softened and said, "Follow me and do what I tell you." We walked along the outside deck and climbed a set of stairs. He stopped outside a door and said, "Wait here." I waited for a few minutes and was at the point of leaving when the door opened and the Steward pulled me in. "Here boy, now's your chance. Talk to him." Without waiting, in case my will failed, I strode forward and asked "Captain, might I have a word with you?" The captain looked at me without recognition and then finally said, "Oh. The stowaway. What do you want boy?" I gulped, "Sir. I have tried to work hard since I came aboard. I would like to return to Rome. May I work my way back to Europe? I will be glad to work in the kitchen again." The captain looked at me and in a cold voice "You made me and my crew look like fools in front of His Majesty stowing away onboard and hiding for two days till we were far at sea. In the old days a stowaway would be thrown overboard without remorse. We don't do that now and you're lucky that the Emperor put you to work with the cook. I would have bound and gagged you and left you in the hold till we got to Mexico. As it is, I can't do that, but you will be turned over to the port police as soon as we dock. If you want to get back to Rome you can walk as far as I'm concerned!" With that he turned from me and a sailor pushed me, not too harshly, out of the room. "Keep your head down and be on your watch," he whispered. "There are people here who would just as soon slit your throat as look at you." As he pushed me out the door he continued, "We should be to Vera Cruz in a few days. The captain means to put you off in chains, but other sailors might try something before then."

I hadn't told Georg anything about what had happened, but this time I felt I needed advice. I sat him down and told him everything, starting with the sailor losing a week's pay to being kicked in the side, and what the captain and second sailor had said. Removing my shirt I showed him my bruised side and asked, "What do you think I should do?" Georg thought for a moment. "Well. The first thing you need to learn is how to defend yourself. But for now don't go out alone till we get to Vera Cruz. When you deliver food to the Emperor make sure you take the main passageways. I suppose some of those sailors would be glad to catch you in the hold when nobody's around so make sure you don't oblige them." He paused in thought. "The Captain means to put you off. That could mean tying you up and giving you to Mexican authorities." That sounded like branding me as a criminal. "You need to avoid that. A criminal in port would have very little rights." He paused again and smiled. "But if you arrived as part of the Emperor's staff they couldn't do anything." I sensed his optimism. "You mean if I tell people I'm working for the Emperor it would be OK?" "No, It doesn't work just like that" came the reply. "You'll need to talk to the Emperor and ask him if you could join his staff. That's your only chance right now."

ON THE ROYAL STAFF

Time was limited. We would be arriving in Vera Cruz within 48 hours. I had to stay away from sailors, yet talk to Emperor to plead my case before the captain had a chance to throw me in chains. The evenings tended to be the time when the Countess and others who were following Maximilian to Mexico gathered on deck to watch the sunset. I took this as my best chance to be on deck and not get caught by a sailor intent on hurting me. Georg and I planned it well. We made snacks and set them up on a tray that I could carry on deck. While there I might have a chance to talk to the Emperor. I put on the best shirt that I could find from the cabinet and carried the tray. At the last second Georg said, "Wait. I'll go with you just in case." The two of us worked our way to the upper deck where a small crowd had gathered. As we climbed one set of stairs the sailor who had kicked me appeared walking down the corridor. He looked like he was about to say something but a look at Georg changed his mind.

We arrived on deck and Georg said, "There. There's everyone who will be going to Mexico. Now's your chance. Good luck." I took the tray and walked through the crowd. I stopped in front of Schertzenlechner to give him a snack and he gave a quick "Thanks" and I continued around the deck. Eloin saw me but gave me a dirty look. I wondered if he had ever been able to clean my vomit out of his clothes. He didn't take a snack. Then the Countess came forward and taking a snack said, "Oh. Leopold, isn't it? Have you enjoyed the voyage? Will you be returning to Europe with the Novara?" I thought it best to answer. "No Countess. I have no money to pay for passage and the captain has no use for hands right now." That was the truth as far as I could tell. I would have to pay for passage back and the captain hadn't offered me work. "Well. What shall you do?" She asked. I paused as if just thinking of it. "Do you suppose the Emperor would take me on as a worker?" She laughed "Well, why don't you ask him? You can't expect him to read your mind! Come! Let's ask." With a quick thumbs up to Georg I followed her over to where the Emperor was standing talking to Eloin. "Your Majesty," said the Countess in a very cultivated voice, "Leopold, whom you might remember, has a question. He would like to work for you in the new Empire. Well. Go ahead Leopold. Don't just stand there tongue tied. Tell him how you have no money to pay for passage and the captain has no need for hands right now." I stepped forward and, bowing deeply, I said, "It's true Your Majesty. I have no money to pay for passage back to Europe and the captain has no need for hands right now. I would count it an honor to work for you in the new Empire. I'm a hard worker and willing to do anything."

At that point Eloin, who had been standing to one side, interjected "Sire. We have enough staff now. There will be many Mexicans who need employment in the new Empire." Maximilian looked as if he were about to agree with Eloin when Schertzenlechner huffed, "Well. I fail to see what a mining engineer knows about our employment needs. Sire. I think we could use him in the household or stables. Not every Mexican can speak German or French that we will need in the Royal household." Maximilian looked like he hated to be stuck in the middle but finally said, "Well. I suppose you're right. We can't expect every Mexican to speak German or French. I guess we can find something for you to do boy, but don't expect much pay." With a huge smile I said, "Thank you Your Majesty. I promise to work hard." Maximilian gave a quick smile and said, "Schertzenlechner. Make sure he gets listed as staff when we disembark. Come Countess. Let's see what is taking the Empress," and with that he walked away. Eloin huffed, "Well. You got your way this time," and stomped away. Schertzenlechner chuckled and said, "Well. You have one enemy now. Meet me at the gangplank as soon as we reach Vera Cruz." I left, happy for the first time in my life that I had vomited on somebody.

I searched for Georg in the crowd on deck, but didn't see him, so continued on down the four decks to the galley. I was so happy about having a chance to work that I didn't pay attention to my surroundings. I was walking down the corridor and from out of the shadows came a fist that connected hard to my chest. It was such a powerful blow that I was knocked across the hall to the opposite wall where I crumpled to the floor. I lay there with my breath knocked out of me as the sailor advanced toward me ready to kick me again. "Cost me pay, you did! I'll beat that out of you!" He pulled back his foot to give a kick and it was just the chance I needed to move my body so that my back was to the wall and his foot whizzed past my head. Thinking of what Georg had said that I needed to learn how to defend myself I grabbed his boot as it went past my head and threw him off balance. He landed with a crash on his back and I jumped on him with a rage unleashed. He was heavier and older than I, but I had the advantage of surprise and I pounded his face while shouting "I will not run! I will survive!" Finally, my rage diminished, I pushed away. I looked at him on the floor. He was breathing hard and bleeding out of what looked like a newly broken nose and from his mouth I saw a gap where a tooth had been. "Are we even?" I asked. He looked at me with respect. "Even." I turned and returned to the galley.

I was bouncing with excitement when I told Georg what had happened, "And then he said, 'even' and I came here." I concluded. Georg smiled. "Well, good. You fought because you had to not because you wanted to. I don't think you need to worry about him for the rest of the voyage. Now you need to start thinking about the future. Who do you know that will be continuing on with the Emperor?" I hadn't really thought what it would be like to leave the ship. It had been my home for over a month now and Georg my only family. I was sad at the prospect of leaving him and still mourning the loss of my family, now on the other side of the globe. "I suppose I know the Countess, Schertzenlechner, and Eloin." I told him how

Schertzenlechner had seemed happy when he found that I had vomited on Eloin. "I don't think they like each other." I concluded. "OK. The temptation would be to cultivate a relationship with one at the expense of the other. Schertzenlechner might really think that they need a German speaker in the household, or he might be doing what he can to irritate the other. My suggestion is not to become involved in their fights. If you do you will end up the loser. Be careful where you put your trust," he concluded. I let it all sink in, "Thank you for what you have done for me. I'm glad I put my trust in you. Now I think I have one more favor to ask. If I write a letter to my father will you post it when you get back to Europe? I want them to know that I am all right." Georg smiled. "I think I can do that."

VERA CRUZ

27 May, 1864

Dear Father and Stepmother.

First let me tell you that I am sorry for everything I did to lose your trust. Maria. I am sorry that I stole your money. I wish I could send you money now, but the truth is I have no money. Second, let me tell you that I am fine and I have matured a lot in the past few weeks. The night I left I had just come from helping my friends, (who I realize now were not true friends) steal money from a house. I left home angry. I was angry at myself, but not angry at you. I went to the waterfront in search of Giovanni and discovered that he had died the day before. At that point I thought that I was being chased by police and I tried to run away. I jumped aboard a ship hoping to hide until the police left and while running I knocked myself out on a beam and lay undiscovered for two days. By that time we were underway with no way of turning back. The ship is the ship that is bringing the Archduke Maximilian of Austria to Mexico to become Emperor. I was able to work in the galley on the voyage across, but because I am a stowaway I am not allowed to return on the same ship and was threatened with imprisonment when we landed in Vera Cruz. Fortunately the Emperor Maximilian has given me employment with the royal household so I will not be turned over as a criminal to port authorities. We

will be disembarking tomorrow in Vera Cruz, Mexico and
this ship will return to Austria. I have asked Georg to post
this letter when he reaches port in Austria and I hope it
finds you well. I don't know what I will be doing for the
Imperial Household but please be assured that I will not do
anything foolish (I have done enough foolish things to last
a lifetime) and I will think of you often. I will write when I
am sure that a letter will reach you. In the meantime I offer
my sincere apologies for how I behaved and I hope to
become a man whom you would be proud to call son.

All my love,

Leopold

I blew on the fresh ink to let it dry. I thought about all
the miles I had traveled to get to this point and all the miles
the letter would have to travel to get back to Rome. I
wondered if they would notice that I hadn't promised to
come home. In truth, I didn't know if I would be able to go
home again. The Emperor did not promise me a big salary
and unless I could work my way across the ocean again it
would take years to earn enough money to pay for passage
to Europe. I folded the paper carefully and put it in an
envelope with my father's address on the outside. "You'll
somehow find a way to post this?" I asked. "Yes boy, I
told you. It will take another six weeks to get to Europe. If
we dock in Civitavecchia I will personally take it to your
father. If we do not go to Rome but to Venice I will find a

way to post it there. Don't worry. Us old sailors find ways to get things done." Counting out the six weeks at a minimum for the letter to get to Europe I wondered what I would be doing in six weeks. I had no idea what I would be doing. I hadn't even seen Schertzenlechner since last night when he had told me to meet him on the gangplank. I had been kept busy belowdecks and wanted to stay away from trouble just in case any other sailors wanted to beat me. I had shouted "I will not run. I will survive," but I wasn't going to go looking for trouble. We should dock in Vera Cruz in the morning and I will stay out of the way till then. I don't think the captain will try to place me in chains now but I plan on not being seen by anybody until I meet Schertzenlechner on the gangplank. By that time it would be too late for anybody to do anything.

I spent a sleepless night thinking about the future and what awaited off the ship. When I awoke from dozing I felt a different motion of the ship and the engines, which had been a constant background hum, sounded different. "Wake up boy," came the voice of Georg from the galley. "The ship will be docking soon and you'll need to be meeting Schertzenlechner. He'll keep you busy I imagine." I looked around at the cabin I used and the galley that had been my home for six weeks. I had grown up a lot in the past few weeks and now it was time to move on. Since I arrived with no luggage I would be leaving with no luggage except a full heart. "Here boy, take this," said Georg as he handed me a pack. "I found some clothes that should fit you and a few other things you might need." I was suddenly overcome with emotion and embraced Georg in fierce hug. "Thank you for everything you've done for me. Thank you for helping me grow up." Georg allowed himself a short hug and then pushed me away with "All right. There you go boy. Time to be going on to your next adventure. Remember old Georg and think before you do something so you don't end up on a ship to Antartica next time!" I tearfully agreed and left the galley with a light heart.

I arrived at the gangplank as the city of Vera Cruz appeared in the distance. The deck felt hot and humid with a breeze coming from the shore. I wondered how hot it would feel when we quit moving. I suddenly felt a sense of fear. "It's so hot and uncomfortable. What will I do? I don't know anything." I hadn't felt this bad since the other night when I cried out, "God, can you fix this?" I heard myself saying, "I will not run. I will survive." A sense of peace came over me as I searched the crowd that had started to gather on deck to take in the sight as the city grew before us. I saw Schertzenlechner and headed in his direction. "There you are boy, when we dock I want you to go out on the pier and find out how many people are waiting to cheer the arrival of the Emperor. The authorities from Mexico City have been notified of our arrival date. Do you speak Spanish…?" "Leo sir," I finished assuming he had forgotten my name. "I know some words from growing up on the docks at home, but I'm not fluent." He replied. "Not to worry now. The authorities from Mexico City will speak German or French so you should be able to communicate if you find them. You'll have to learn Spanish if you are going to work here. His Imperial Majesty will need all the support he can get. He and Her Imperial Majesty Charlotte have been studying since he was asked to become Emperor." I saw some sailors approaching the crowd gathering on the deck. One of the sailors carried chains and I suddenly became worried. "Sir. I'm afraid the captain might want to throw me in chains and turn me over to port authorities as a stowaway. " In the distance I could see the captain standing keeping an eye my direction. "No. The Emperor has set you as part of the Imperial Household staff." The sailors came toward me and one grabbed me roughly, "Here boy. Now you'll get yours for stowing away aboard an Austrian Naval ship." The other sailor started to attach the manacles to my wrists when Schertzenlechner said in a rather loud voice, "What is the meaning of this? What are you doing to a member of the Royal Household? The Emperor will hear of this!" At this the sailors paused for only a moment but one said, looking in the direction of the captain, "Sorry sir, we are only following orders." Again Schertzenlechner said just a little louder "The Emperor will hear of this! Where is the captain? I demand to see the captain!" At this the captain had no choice but to enter. "Good morning Mr. Schertzenlechner. What seems to be the problem? I hope this criminal isn't bothering you? I shall be turning him over to port authorities for stowing away. They shall take care of it promptly so it doesn't bother your entourage." Schertzenlechner said with exaggerated politeness "There must be some mistake captain. Your sailors are trying to arrest a member of the Imperial Household and one of Her Majesty's favorites. Certainly you don't want to upset the Emperor as he enters his new realm? Perhaps your men are mistaking this man for another who stowed away?" At the mention of the Emperor the captain flushed and knew that he had lost. "Yes, perhaps. Release him," he said to the sailors as Schertzenlechner turned to leave. Under his breath he whispered, "Run far from me. If I see you again I'll throw you overboard myself." One of the sailors gave me a wink as he pulled the chains from my wrists.

The gangplank dropped on the dock and I was the first person to enter the Empire of Mexico as a representative of His Royal Highness Maximiliano, Emperador de México. I walked down the pier expecting to see crowds and banners welcoming the arriving Emperor, but I saw nothing. It seemed like a normal day on the waterfront, like any I had seen in Civitavecchia all my life. I continued up the waterfront in search of anybody who seemed like an official of the government or the port. Finally I saw one man who looked official and introduced myself as a representative of the Emperor and asked him where the crowds to greet the Emperor were. The man looked like he doubted somebody my age was a representative of the Emperor but didn't argue with me. "The delegation from

Mexico City hasn't arrived yet. We have a tent set up to greet the Emperor and there shall be a banquet in their honor when the delegation from Mexico City arrives." We talked as we walked up the dock and he pointed out the tent in the distance. "Tell me. You're not really a representative of the Emperor, are you, How old are you?" "Sixteen," I replied. "Mr. Schertzenlechner, personal secretary to the Emperor, made me a member of the Royal Household staff and asked me to check on the status of the arrival ceremony." The man smiled and introduced himself as "Juarez. No relation. Port director. For now everybody will have to wait for the arrival of the delegation." I didn't know what he meant by "Juarez. No relation." It seemed to be a joke that I wasn't in on. I returned to the ship, and finding Schertzenlechner, I reported "The delegation from Mexico City hasn't arrived yet. The city does have a tent and banquet ready for the arrival ceremony. The port director a Mr. Juarez said for now everybody has to wait." Schertzenlechner chuckled at the name. "Please sir. What is so funny about his name? He said, 'Juarez, no relation' and laughed." Schertzenlechner laughed again. "There's no reason you would know. Benito Juarez is the pretend president of Mexico. We shall be fighting him to proclaim the Empire."

I was astonished. I thought that Maximilian was coming to a land eager for his arrival. Now I'm told that we have to fight a war. I didn't have time to think about it. I was sent to check out the tent and report back to

Schertzenlechner if it would be large enough for the near one hundred people who were traveling with Maximilian. He added, "Find out how they are planning on getting us to Mexico City? I don't want to travel by donkey through the wilderness." I left the ship again in search of Juarez and found him near the tent. "Oh yes. There will be ample room for His Majesty and the group from the Novara. Whenever His Majesty wishes to leave Vera Cruz the train will be waiting." That sounded promising and I returned to tell my supervisor. "Well. It's good to know we have arrived where there is proper transportation at least. Go on now and scout out the arrival of the group from Mexico City and report back to me. His Majesty will want to know as soon as they arrive so they can be greeted on the ship. He will not set foot on Mexican soil until he has received the delegation on board ship."

I left the ship again wondering how many times I would do that before we all left. It was hot and humid in the early afternoon. I wondered how people could stand to live here. The dock now seemed deserted and I felt like I was the only one walking along the waterfront. I saw a woman napping under an awning, a basket full of some kind of food at her side. She must have sensed me standing there and roused herself enough to say, "Te gusta?" I remembered enough Spanish to know that she asked me if I liked it. I, of course, had no idea what it was and didn't know how to ask so I just smiled. She said something again that I didn't understand so I just smiled again.

Finally she pointed at her palm and held up three fingers. I assumed that whatever she was selling cost three something. I didn't even know what kind of money they used here. Since I had no money I just shrugged my shoulders and pulled at my pockets to signify that I had no money and walked on with a smile. I saw more and more people napping in the shade and finally decided that they were doing what we did at home: napping during the heat of the day after lunch. To me it looked wonderful. It was so hot and a nap in the shade sounded so relaxing. Unfortunately I hadn't found any information about the delegation from Mexico City so I set aside the idea of a nap and continued searching for anybody who would know about arrivals from out of town. Finally I saw Mr. Juarez under an awning in front of what looked like a port office. I hesitated to wake him but he spoke without opening his eyes, "Leopold now is the time for siesta. Come have a tamale and take a siesta. The delegates won't arrive during the heat of the day. Nobody will do heavy work during the heat of the day. Everybody is taking their siesta" I looked at the food and suddenly felt hungry and had my first meal and siesta in Mexico. An hour later he stirred and said, "Come Leopold. Let's see if we can find any news about the arrival of the delegation." We walked along the waterfront and he explained that they would be coming from the highlands outside of town so we just needed to see if we could see any coaches coming from outside of town. The arrival of any coach would signify the arrival of the delegates.

We didn't have long to wait, "Look. See in the distance there the cloud of dust from the hill. For sure it is the delegation arriving from Mexico City. Go back and tell the Emperor that the delegation will arrive in around ninety minutes." I ran back to the ship, and reported to Schertzenlechner. He said, "Well that will be too late I believe for the formal landing. We will receive the delegation here on the ship and make the formal celebration tomorrow. Go tell Juarez to direct them to the ship when they arrive and then run ahead of them when they arrive to warn us." I did as I was told and left the ship again. We sat near the port entrance and when we saw the coaches pull through the gate Juarez walked out to meet them and I ran back to the ship to announce the arrival.

The deck was prepared for the meeting with many of the people who had sailed with Maximilian and Charlotte gathered in small groups waiting for the Emperor. The Emperor and Empress came from their cabin as several coaches pulled up to the bottom of the gangplank. The captain, now all smiles, greeted the arrivals on deck and presented them to the Royal couple. It was at this point I realized that the Mexican idea of court formality would be different from the Austrian. A man was introduced to Maximilian and instead of bowing as I had done several times a day for the past six weeks grabbed the Emperor by his hand in a crushing handshake. A woman gave the

Empress a hug as if they were sisters and pulled out a cigarette and motioned as if offering one to the Empress. The royal couple looked shocked but quickly covered it up with smiles. The reception didn't last long. Maximilian gave a few words in Spanish that I didn't understand and the delegation left. Schertzenlechner came up behind me and said, "The formal arrival will take place early tomorrow morning. Make sure the tent is safe for the ceremony." I took this to mean that I should pass the night in the tent so I took five minutes and ran back down to the galley to say goodbye to Georg. "I know I said goodbye this morning but now I have a chance again." I told him quickly what I had done and what had happened on the upper deck. He frowned, "They are not ready for an Empire here. Mark my words. This will end poorly. Watch your back and always keep an escape route available." I promised and with another embrace I left the ship for the last time and went to the tent prepared to pass the night there.

I arrived at the tent and looked around in the dark and decided there was really nothing I could do. Since I had slept so little the previous night and had been running all day I stretched out on the ground and with my pack as a pillow I fell fast asleep. I don't know how long I had been asleep but a storm came up and started whipping the sides of the tent. Since I was now wide awake I got up and walked around the area. The wind was picking up and soon the decorations that had been set up to honor the Imperial couple were knocked to the ground before the Emperor had even had a chance to see them. As I huddled back in the tent I hoped that this was not an omen of things to come.

Early in the morning before sunrise I made my way back to the ship to report the destruction. Schertzenlechner took the report. "The Emperor and Empress are taking Mass in the main cabin. We will depart shortly." Not knowing what else to do I waited for the departure. The man who had greeted the Emperor with a handshake the night before arrived and I heard him say, "We won't waste any time here with the illness spreading. We will leave today by train." We passengers and crew all gathered at the foot of the gangplank and cheered as Maximilian and Charlotte took their first steps on Mexican soil. They walked up the dock to the tent prepared for celebration and past the destroyed decorations. If they thought it was a bad omen they didn't say anything. There were no locals there to cheer the new monarch. It was too early for people to be out of bed. Charlotte had a smile on her face as she boarded the train and we were off on the next part of the adventure.

The imperial couple, of course, had seats on the train. The seats looked narrow and uncomfortable: hardly suitable for an Emperor. I found no seat and continued through the car to the next one. It was full also with people standing in the aisle packed tight. I turned and started to go back to the first car and a sound above my head forced my attention up. "Aqui," came a voice. "Subite!"

TO MEXICO CITY

I knew the word 'aqui.' It means 'here.' I decided that 'subite' meant 'climb up' since the voice came from above and I saw a ladder. By this time the train had started to move and I really had no choice so up I climbed. At the top of the ladder I discovered about twenty people riding on top of each car. The voice continued saying something I didn't understand but I saw now it was attached to a boy about my own age. He didn't look European, although he had dark hair and brown eyes like many Spaniards I had seen, his face had a brown complexion. I decided that I had met a true Mexican. "Como te llamas?" He asked, holding out his hand. Again I knew the question, and replied "Leopold," and then since I didn't know what else to say fell silent. By this time the train had picked up speed and conversation, aside from the language barrier, became difficult. "Diego," he shouted, pointing at himself. I shook his hand and smiled again, but could do no more because of the noise.

We sat on top of the moving car and although the breeze made by the moving car cooled the temperature, the smoke drifting back from the engine made the trip less than comfortable. Diego shouted once, "Hace calor," which I took to mean that it was hot, and we continued in silence.

Finally the train slowed as we started up the hills outside Vera Cruz. With the breeze coming from the mountains it pushed the smoke away from the train. With the train slowing it became possible to speak and Diego looked at me and said, "Austria?" I assumed he was asking me if I was Austrian and I said, "No." "Ahh," he smiled. "Francais!" "No" I replied again, for even though the French controlled Civitavecchia, we did not consider ourselves French. "From Rome. Papa." Finally he said in French, "You speak French?" Although in Civitavecchia we spoke our own dialect of Italian most of us knew French because of the occupation. "Yes." I replied. "The French occupy my city so I can speak some French." He smiled "The French occupy Mexico so I speak some French too." That surprised me. I knew that there were some French soldiers on the ship, but I didn't know that it occupied Mexico. That must be why Georg had said that Napoleon had asked Maximilian to be emperor. I wondered what else I would find out about this new country. "Why are you here if you are not French or Austrian?" I laughed. "That's a funny story" and told him the whole story about trying to escape from the police and ending up a stowaway onboard the ship. He laughed, "But it must be hard to be away from your family?" And then, as if sensing my emotions, "There must be many things you wish you could tell them now. I am trying to get back to my family too, but nothing as exciting as that. I have been in Vera Cruz over two years now while the fighting has been going on. Now I think it will be safe to get to Mexico City and from there maybe I can get home." "Where's home?" I asked. "It's a city called Guanajuato in the middle of the country. I came here with my mother over two years ago to visit her side of the family. She died a few months ago of the sickness that is bad in Vera Cruz. Now I shall try to get home to my father and family." I felt sorry for him that he hadn't been home for two years and sorry again that his mother had died. I guess we were more alike than different.

At that moment the train started to slow and pretty soon it stopped in what looked like a small village. Obviously it wasn't Mexico City. Diego looked at me. "From here there are only coaches, horses, or shoes. This is the end of the train line." I heard some commotion from below as people heard that they would now be forced to change. I descended the ladder and found Schertzenlechner telling the Emperor, "Your Majesty. This is the end of the rail line. From here the delegates have arranged coaches to take us the rest of the way. We shall pass the night here, but unfortunately there are no accommodations for everybody in our group so we must split up and let some go ahead quickly while we take our time and visit smaller villages. The Countess has agreed to lead the first group as she is —ah— more adventurous and up to a challenge than others." he concluded tactfully. "Wonderful," replied the Emperor. "have you seen the flowers? They are beautiful. You won't find those in Austria. Well Leo! What do you think?" He questioned me as he saw me standing near Schertzenlechner. Surprised that he remembered me I said It's beautiful Sire. I'm looking forward to seeing the rest of the country." "See it you shall! We shall turn this country in to a paradise!" He said as he strode away from us and off to his accommodations. Schertzenlechner looked at me and ordered "I want you in charge of making sure that each person gets their own luggage in their own coach. We will not be spending the next few nights together. In fact, The Countess will arrive in Mexico City before we do. You!" He said, pointing at Diego. "Help him." If Diego thought about saying that he wasn't part of the Royal household he didn't show it, but went right to work and we spent nearly two hours matching luggage to guests. With a crack of whips the coaches taking the Countess and the others were off on their fast trip to Mexico City. We would go slower so that Maximilian and Charlotte would have more time to meet their new subjects. We had some time to look around after the Countess had left and I wanted to see what I had heard while we were unloading the train, that this was an Indian village. I had never really heard of Indians, but they sounded exotic. I wondered if they ate people and wore skins. I asked Diego, "Where are the Indians?" He looked at me with a strange look. "Indians? They are everywhere. I'm part Indian. The people in the village are probably full blooded Indians. That's why I look different from you. My ancestors came from Spain and married Indians. Our president is full blooded Indi…" He stopped as if he hadn't meant to say the last part. "Your president?" I said. "But you have an emperor. You just saw him two hours ago." Diego looked like he wanted to be anywhere but here.

"Yes. Of course." But didn't sound too convincing. He was saved as we heard the Empress nearly shout with pleasure. "Oh how wonderful, this is so beautiful." We walked over and saw that the Indians had built a flowered arch for the Royal couple to go through on the way to the coach. Both the Emperor and Empress looked nearly overwhelmed with emotion at what the Indians had done for them. "Oh." I heard the Empress whisper. "What gracious, simple people. I've never seen such kindness before." The Indians picked up a cheer of "Viva el Imperador" as Maximilian and Charlotte went through the arch. I looked at the happy couple and was proud of them and happy that I could be a part of bringing stability to this country. I glanced at Diego, but he looked angry. I was going to ask him what was wrong, but the order came. "Get the luggage settled for everybody staying here!" The Countess had left with her group and we would stay here. The elite went off to hotels or homes and Diego and I searched for a place to sleep, finally settling for benches in one of the coaches.

The next morning I woke sore and Diego looked in pain as he pulled himself up from the floor of the coach. "The bench was narrow and I fell off sometime in the night." He said. We scouted the area and without finding any food we decided that we would be going hungry. I looked at the coaches that were ready to go and Diego looked at me. "What did I tell you? From here on it's coaches, horses or shoes. It looks like we have shoes!" He was right. All the coaches were full of the elite of the new Empire. We would be walking. Fortunately we could walk just as fast as the donkeys so we had a chance to talk. "Why did you look angry when the Indians were shouting?" I asked. Diego paused for a minute. "The Indians have a belief that a blond man will come from beyond the seas to save them." He pointed at the lead coach. "Look at the blond man. It is the same thing that happened when Cortez came from Spain and we were under foreign occupation for hundreds of years." I had heard of Cortez discovering Mexico, but I guess he wasn't very popular here. Diego continued. "I will tell you the story sometime of my grandfather and the war for freedom. It's the story my grandfather never gets tired of telling. He is a legend in my family. I miss him so much." I wanted to ask him to tell me more, but decided he would tell me in his time. Instead I told him about Giovanni and Georg and how I missed them. I was just in the midst of the story about beating up the sailor while shouting "I will not run. I will survive," when the skies opened and rain came down in torrents. Diego howled in laughter. "Welcome to the rainy season! It will be like this till after 'The Grito!' Oh we need the rain." He seemed happy that it was raining. We soon were kept busy pushing the coaches as the trails turned to mud and I didn't have a chance to ask him what 'The Grito' was. We continued on till nearly 2:00 AM before we saw the lights of Cordoba. As if on cue the rains stopped and the coaches were surrounded by Indians shouting "Viva el Imperador" as we entered town.

It seemed as if every person in town had come out in the middle of the night to greet Maximilian and Charlotte. I was caught up in the excitement and shouted "Viva" with everybody. I glanced over at Diego and he was quiet with a hint of a smile on his face. Eventually the shouting died down and the crowds disappeared and we were left to find shelter. The Emperor and Empress had been invited to a home but the rest of us were left to our own devices. Diego and I thought about spending the rest of the short night in one of the coaches, but finally spread our packs on the floor of the stables and slept with the horses.

After a few hours we were up again and hungry. So far on this trip we had eaten leftovers from the elite or nothing at all. This morning we were lucky. The men driving the mules shared their huge breakfast with us and we went to work on full stomachs making sure that the traveling party had their luggage. With a crack of whips the 'arrieros' led the mules out on the trip. It would take another night or two for us to reach Puebla.

Again there was no room in the coaches so Diego and I decided that we would be walking all the way to Mexico City. The roads were little more than tracks running through the jungle and sometimes when it rained the tracks became flooded with mud and we had to unload the coaches to lighten the load and push the coach through to dry ground. The 'arrieros' and Diego and I joked through each detour and I picked up more Spanish words. I wondered if the Countess was having as much fun as we were.

While we hit a dry stretch of road and didn't have to work we had a chance to talk and walk. "Why have you spent so long in Vera Cruz?" I asked "Since your family lives far away." He paused in thought. "We wouldn't have been able to travel while my mother was sick and it has been too dangerous to travel since the battle of Puebla." "Battle of Puebla?" I asked. "There's been a battle where we are going?" Diego continued. "The French have been here in Mexico as long as I can remember because they say that Mexico owes money to Europe. Two years ago this month. No. Last month. It's June now. Two years ago last month on the Cinco de Mayo the French surrounded Puebla and there was a big battle. There were many more French soldiers than Mexican soldiers, but by the end of the day the Mexicans had won and the French were forced to retreat. Since then it has been too dangerous to travel with bandits trying to control the roads to Vera Cruz." I asked "So who have you been living with since your mother died?" Diego grimaced. "The Vomito Negro has killed so many people. The black death kills many people along the coast. I've been living with different family members from my mother's side ever since she died. I've stayed a few weeks with one cousin and time here and there with other cousins. We Mexicans would never let family starve or go without a home but now without my mother, uncle and grandparents I decided to go back to Guanajuato and live with my father. My cousin heard that Maximiliano would be coming to Vera Cruz and knew that he would have lots of security to Mexico City. He helped me get through the guards by the train and I jumped up and rode the roof. That's when I saw you and had you come up with me." I laughed "Wait! You mean to tell me that you were a stowaway too?" I think we are brothers now! Diego laughed too. "That's why I was very quick to help when the man told me to help. I figured that if I looked like a worker they couldn't really throw me off the train! Once I get to Mexico City I'll try to find a way to get to Guanajuato." I had an idea. "If you continue to work with us Schertzenlechner will have to let you continue. Maybe he'll just think that you're part of the staff. At any rate be good to him or Eloin. They seem to have the most power: besides Charlotte, of course." We continued on walking and laughing and spent two nights on the road to Puebla. By the third day we were glad to see sunshine and the buildings of Puebla in the distance. "See." Diego said, "You can see the city from all around. We were able to see the French and beat them here!" I wondered why we were stopping in Puebla if it was such an important city for the rebels and was even more surprised when we got there to cheering crowds. French soldiers were everywhere and it was a party atmosphere. At the gates to the city a man came, and kneeling before the royal couple said, "Welcome to Puebla and feliz cumpleaños Emperatriz!"

Then we realized it was Charlotte's birthday and the French had arranged a big party. For the first time in several days we had nothing to do as everybody in the coaches scattered off to various homes and hotels. We were left with the mule drivers who shared some food with us in the stables. Eventually Eloin came with a keg of rum and said, "Her Majesty commands that we drink a toast in her honor! Viva Emperatriz!" and left us with the keg to return to the party. We were each able to get one drink to toast Her Majesty before the keg ran out and the mule drivers were forced to find another place to celebrate. Again Diego and I were left alone in the stables. "Do you think you'll be able to find a way to Guanajuato once we get to Mexico City?" I asked. "I'm sure there's something." He replied. "There's always traffic to Queretaro and from there I should be able to find my way." The cities meant nothing to me so I'm not sure how far they were from Mexico City. It didn't sound like it would be an easy trip. "But it doesn't matter. As long as I'm moving forward I'm happy. Grandfather Diego said that when we left Guanajuato we were recreating the trip Rodrigo took 50 years ago so now I'm doing it in reverse." I was going to ask him who Rodrigo was, but at that moment Eloin came back. "You boys come here. The Emperor wants all the employees of the household to toast Her Majesty on her birthday." We worked our way up to a ballroom filled with French soldiers, Mexican elites, the members of the household and the royal couple. We were each given a glass of champagne and Maximilian lifted his glass and said, "To Carlota," and the crowd responded with "Carlota." Maximilian and Carlota left but the party continued. I looked at Diego and said, "I guess you are an employee of the house now. Eloin wanted all household employees here!" Diego grinned. "See. I'm moving forward."

Eventually we moved back to the stables and pulled our packs again to make beds in the straw. I dreamed that night of Maximilian shouting "We're moving forward!" while Diego was shouting "Back to Vera Cruz. Escape to Vera Cruz with Rodrigo." I woke with a start to only hear the snores of Diego and the sniffing of the mules.

After a couple days rest in Puebla we started the journey to Mexico City. From here we would start climbing the mountains and it would be hard work without a coach. Maximilian continued to be happy in noticing all the flowers. When we walked close to his coach we heard him telling Charlotte about his journeys to South America and the flowers he had seen there. I didn't mean to listen in to what he was saying but my ears perked up when Charlotte said, "All the flowers of the world won't make up for what your brother did. We should release the letter." I thought for a moment about what I had heard on the ship so long ago. They must have written a letter about their disagreements with the Austrian emperor and now Charlotte wanted to release it to the public. I stepped back away from the coach and told Diego a little about the family history. Diego replied, "I don't think President Juarez will step down without a fight. He has left Mexico City and gone north, but there are too many rebels around the country for Maximilian to fight. Look at Puebla. There were many people cheering him last night, but two years ago the French lost." I had to agree that it looked difficult. "If he had to give up all claims in Austria he will never leave here. He couldn't go back." I finished.

The climb from Puebla was difficult for the mules and more difficult for two teenage boys and we had little chance to talk for the next two days. We fell down exhausted at the end of each day and hoped that we would arrive soon in Mexico City. Finally three days out from Puebla we could see the buildings of Mexico City in the distance. Diego told me a little of the history of the city.

"The story goes that the Aztecs left their home country in the North in search of a new homeland. In their ancient mythology they had a story that their journey would be over when they saw an eagle eating a snake. As they arrived in the middle of the valley they saw an island with an eagle sitting on a cactus eating a snake. They knew that the prophecy had been fulfilled and they set up their new homeland on the island." I asked, "Is the lake still there?" "No." came the reply. "The city has grown and the lake has been drained as people have come. It's a much larger city now." "How well do you know it?" I asked. "Not very. My mother and I spent a few days here when we went to visit her family in Vera Cruz, but we always hear stories about the old days," he continued. "Do you know about Cortes?" He asked. I had only heard the name a couple times on the ship so I didn't know anything. "Hernan Cortes was a Spaniard who came on a voyage of discovery from Spain. When he got to Vera Cruz in 1521 he was afraid that his sailors would mutiny so he had his ship set on fire so that his men would be forced to follow him." I laughed at the idea of Cortes destroying ships to get his soldiers in line. "Don't laugh. It worked," said Diego. "He forced his men to climb from Vera Cruz to what is now Mexico City just as we are doing. He arrived and the people thought he was a god returned from the past. Montezuma the Emperor allowed him in to the city built on the lake." I questioned, "So the lake was still there then?" "Yes. The lake was there and the island city was connected to the mainland by bridges. Montezuma let them enter the city when perhaps he should have destroyed the bridges and fought the Spaniards." "So was there a battle?" I questioned. "Not right away. Montezuma wasn't too sure if Cortes was a god or not. If he was a god he didn't want to upset him. Finally in the end Cortes ordered a battle and the Empire was over and Montezuma was killed." I was so interested in the story that I suddenly had a thought. "So all those Indians this week who were shouting and cheering?" The reply came back quickly. "Yes. They might still remember the stories of a blond god coming from across the seas to save them. Of course they are not remembering what happened the last time they trusted the one who came from across the seas," he concluded with a laugh.

Schertzenlechner announced to the coaches in a loud voice that was spread up and down the train. "We will be spending the night near the shrine to the Virgin of Guadalupe so that their Majesties may pray and attend Mass at the shrine. Tomorrow we will make the grand entrance to the city!" Again I was confused. "Who is the Virgin of Guadalupe?" I whispered. "She's the Patron Saint of Mexico and Queen of the Americas," came the reply. "You've never heard of her?" Of course I knew about Mary, Mother of God. My mother taught me the rosary when I was just a little boy. "Well," started Diego. "A long time ago when the Church was new in Mexico there was a man named Juan Diego. He was going to the fields one day and he was surprised by a vision of the Virgin. She told him to go tell the Bishop to build a church for her there. Juan Diego did, but the Bishop didn't believe him. When he came back to the same site the Virgin asked him if he had done it. Juan said that he had but that the Bishop didn't believe him. Mary told him to open his tilma, or jacket, and when Juan Diego returned to the Bishop and opened his tilma it was full of roses." I finished, "So that time the Bishop believed?" Diego laughed. "Yes. So we have a shrine here now and we will stop there. "I think I will ask the Virgin to pray for my father in Guanajuato and my mother in heaven. You pray to her too. She's the mother of Jesus. She will talk to Him for you!" I thought for a minute. Certainly my life hadn't been going too well with me trying to do things by myself. Maybe it was time to ask God to help me. "I think you're right." I said. "I'll need all the help I can get in this new country."

The church was crowded with all the notables of Mexico City come to greet the new Emperor. Diego and I managed to stand at the very back of the church to see Maximilian and Charlotte pray and take Communion from the Bishop. While they were praying I spent some time in prayer too, asking for help in this new country and forgiveness for what I had done to get here.

The streets around the shrine were full of shouting "Viva el emperador," "Viva Maximiliano!" "Viva Carlota!" We were going to wander around the outskirts of the city while the Royal Couple went on to a banquet, but we were caught, "Tomorrow the royal couple shall take a train the rest of the way to the palace," announced Schertzenlechner. "Tomorrow morning early I want you two to leave early before the streets are too crowded and get to the palace to start unloading. It's too busy tonight to leave and the streets will be crowded tomorrow when the family leaves." He looked at Diego. "I suppose this means you are on the payroll too," and gave each of us some coins. We looked at each other with happiness. Our first pay as employees of the emperor was spent on tamales in the street.

The next morning we were up from our spot in the stable before dawn. The mule drivers had left yesterday after we had arrived. We were alone with two wagons and two horses and a mountain of luggage. Schertzenlechner had given us a note to introduce us to the palace guard, if there was one, other than that we were on our own to load the luggage and find our way to the palace. "Do you know how to tie the wagon to the horse?" I asked Diego. He laughed. "It's called 'harnessing' a horse," he replied. "Here. You put on this bridle and then we attach the wagon. I haven't done it in a long time but I think I remember. We should get the wagons loaded first though." We worked quickly and the sun was just coming over the horizon when we set out for the palace. We got through the outskirts of town and soon Diego said, "Here. This is the Zocolo. I remember this. The palace is nearby." "Zocolo," I said. "What's that?" "It's the central square. It's where the Aztccs first came. Maybe here you can find the eagle eating a snake." He joked. We continued on till we got to one end of the giant square. "That must be the palace." I said, pointing at a large square building. "That's right. I don't know anything about it though." replied Diego. "Where's the letter? I think we'll need it." Since we had no idea of what to do we just drove the horses right up to the front door. A guard started to tell us to get away and we had to show him our letter. "OK. Take the horses around the back and you'll find a courtyard to unload."

We worked our way around the back, passing by a large church. "This must be the main church," I said. "It's the largest we've seen so far. "I think it is," replied Diego. "Oh. Look. There's the courtyard we need to use." We passed through the courtyard where only one guard was on duty. We asked about locations to put the luggage, but he had no idea. "I just stand guard." He said, pointing in to the house. Since we had no idea where anybody would stay we went on a tour of inspection through the palace. It looked like some people had come in to clean and had only worked a few hours before leaving. Some furniture looked like it had been cleaned and dusted, while other rooms had sheets over furniture and chandeliers covered with cloth to protect from dust. "I don't think the Emperor or Empress will be too happy when they see this." I said. "No. It doesn't look very clean, and I've seen cockroaches while we've been walking. Why don't we set up a table near the front entrance for most of the luggage and we can take the Royal Family's bags upstairs to the suite of rooms that looks like it might be theirs" he suggested. I thought that was a good idea. We really had no idea where anybody would be sleeping and it looked like there was a shortage of beds anyway. We brought any bag that was marked with the royal seal up to a series of rooms facing the Zocolo that we assumed was the royal suite. "We'll have to tell them when they get here," I said, "but you're right. This is the best option, and we can mark the tables downstairs with the names on the bags. We worked most of the morning and as we finished we could hear cheers in the distance and we knew that the Emperor was coming. Soon the guards opened the doors, but it was not the Emperor who entered, but a crowd of what we assumed were the notables of Mexico City. Diego and I stayed in the shadows while the new arrivals gathered to await the Emperor. Again the guards opened the doors facing the Zocolo and we could see Maximilian and Charlotte walking across the Zocolo with cheers ringing around them. They walked through the doors, and if they were disappointed in what they saw, they showed no emotion. Maximilian greeted the notables in the central room where we had set up the tables and then walked upstairs to the balcony with Charlotte, where together they greeted the crowds. "Viva el Emperador, Viva la Imperatriz" were the shouts. Charlotte was glowing with pride as she waved, while Maximilian looked humbled as he stared across the Zocolo filled with his new subjects.

SETTING UP THE EMPIRE

Maximilian and Charlotte went to the balcony numerous times throughout the day to appear before the crowds. In the evening there were fireworks in the Zocolo and it seemed as if the crowds would never leave. Diego and I had spent the day moving boxes and helping the new occupants find rooms. The one thing that hadn't changed was the cleanliness of the house. If anything it looked worse than when we had arrived in the morning. In the morning we had arrived with excitement about being in a royal palace. Now after working all we saw was dust, lice, and the occasional cockroach. "Oh," said Diego, as he killed another cockroach. "I hate cockroaches. I always have. The scorpions at home in Guanajuato I don't mind, but cockroaches are just ugly." I agreed. "I wonder how long it has been since somebody lived here?" I mused. "I don't know," Diego replied. "There has been such turmoil in the government I don't know the last time anybody lived here. I think the crowds have died down and it's not as noisy anymore. Do you think we could actually find a place to sleep now? I don't think we've stopped working since we got here this morning." Since it was now nearly 3:00 AM we had been working round the clock. "Yes" I agreed, "let's find someplace to sleep. Anyplace but the stables. I'm tired of sleeping with horses or donkeys." We had been working upstairs near the royal apartments and talking quietly so as not to disturb Their Majesties in case they were sleeping. Suddenly from behind a closed door we heard a shout. "Lice in the bed. I'm sleeping on the billiard table!" Even the new Emperor of Mexico had problems finding a place to sleep. We laughed as we went downstairs to wrap ourselves in sheets in a hallway.

The following days brought more work and a little more order out of chaos. I began to place names with faces of people who came around the palace. I think the first person I noticed was the French general Bazaine. He came nearly everyday at first to report to the Emperor. Diego told me that he had been in Mexico for a long time "Right now he's been in charge for two years and has been a strong commander. He's killed a lot of rebels but has made things work. There's a telegraph in Vera Cruz now and a train too. The tax office is in Vera Cruz so that's why he makes sure that things work there. Napoleon wants him to collect taxes so that Europe can be repaid."

The Countess Kollonitz, of course, was a regular part of palace life. She seemed to thrive on the adventures of life in a palace that seemed at times European elegance and at times a third class hotel on the point of decay. One evening Diego and I had finished work for the day and had made our way to the kitchens to see if we could find some food. We had just managed to beg some tamales from the cook when we heard a slam at the back kitchen door facing the courtyard where we had first unloaded the luggage. "There you are! Quick! Come with me both of you." She nearly shouted as she ran from the kitchen toward the store rooms. We thought that she needed some help moving something and started to follow, "I can't believe how the French officers could be so stupid." She said while running. "I hope you boys know how to dance." She said while slowing down in front of a store room door. "Can you imagine that?" She questioned anybody and nobody. "Inviting only the young Mexican women and none of the older ones." She continued while searching in the store room. "They left out some of the most important people of the country." She finally held up some dress trousers and jackets. "Well. Hurry up. Get those clothes off now and put these on! Haven't you understood a word I said?" When I started to protest she said, "Come on now! You have nothing I haven't seen after raising three boys. We have to get you dressed and over to the Ball before the presentations and dancing starts. You need to come to the ball to balance out the number of men and women." So that is how Diego and I came to be standing in our underwear with the Countess in a storage room.

We arrived in the ballroom at the National Theatre down the street a few minutes later. I have to admit that we came off looking pretty good, and wondered if we could pass for high class Mexicans. We were each paired with a French woman older than us by two. It was then I realized that we were to be presented to the Emperor and Empress. The Countess had disappeared but Schertszenlechner was acting as head of household and presented each couple. "Mr. Gonzalez and Miss Sanchez de Taigle" he said as Diego approached the royal couple. The Empress, with just a slight smile said, "So pleased to make your acquaintance Miss Sanchez, Mr. Gonzalez." Next was my turn paired with "Miss Maria Juventus and Mr. Fiori." And again this time the Emperor held out his hand while I bowed and Maria curtseyed. "So good to see you" and we were through the receiving line and on the dance floor. When we had tried to protest, in our underwear, that we didn't know how to dance, the Countess had said, "Nonsense. Just do what others are doing." To my surprise I found that I rather enjoyed trying to dance. If the women thought we couldn't dance they didn't say anything. We danced around the ballroom for a few minutes and I noticed General Bazaine follow with his eyes the "date" of Diego. Finally he came over and cut in with a "May I have this dance?" to which, of course, Diego gave up. Then, instead of going to the side, he cut in on me and said with a smile "I would be honored to have this dance?" I was left alone on the sidelines and as my eyes followed the dancers around the ballroom floor I heard the General say, "Forgive me for being so forward, but may I say that you remind me so much of my wife who has been dead for a year now?" If the girl thought he was forward she never said as they continued the dance. Later as we were moving to the dining hall for dinner the General approached the Emperor, "Begging Your Majesty's indulgence. May I have permission to not sit at the royal table but join Maria for dinner?" If the Emperor was upset he didn't show it and only said with a wink. "Of course! I believe you will have much better company than with me. Come Mr. Fiori. It looks like your date has been stolen away from you and you shall have to sit at table with the Empress and I." I froze in fear, but The Empress, sensing my fear, said, "Why yes, Mr. Fiori, Since you share the same name as my dear father we must talk." And she allowed me to escort her to the table. "If my mother could see me now." I thought, and gave Diego a wink.

Sometime around 2:00 AM we were allowed to leave and the Countess was beaming. "There, the first Ball went off well, but the next time we must not allow the French officers to be in charge of invitations. Just because they are paying for the occupation doesn't mean they should leave out some of the most important people in the land." She joined us in the kitchens to finish the tamales that we hadn't had a chance to eat. "Those poor servants from Austria for Her Majesty don't understand Spanish and feel lost here. I wouldn't be surprised if many of them left to return to Austria" I wondered if I would ever get home.

As the weeks passed I began to feel more comfortable in the palace. It was finally starting to look nice and I could sleep through the night now without fear of waking up with bedbugs or cockroaches. Diego and I shared a room in the attic on the opposite side of the palace from the Emperor's suite. "At least we don't have cockroaches up here in the attic." He had said. "True. I hadn't thought that the good thing about being two floors away from a bathroom and having to carry water and a chamber pot up and down three flights of stairs was a good thing, but I suppose you're right."

Another good thing about being in the attic was that we were far away from the bells near the kitchen that summoned servants to the Imperial suite or any other room that had the pull cord hanging by the door. There was a board near the kitchen that had a bell for each room of the Imperial Suites plus bells for numerous other rooms that made up the palace. Since we weren't part of the butler or maid staff we didn't have to sit near the bell on the chance that one of the elites would need something.

What we did get to do, at least one of us, was go riding with the Emperor or the Empress. The first time we got to do this was several weeks in to the Empire. We were working polishing the metal work on one of the carriages that the Empress liked to take on her rides around town. Eloin came out from the palace and said, "Get the carriage ready. Her Majesty wishes to take a ride this afternoon." We quickly finished polishing and got the horse ready but no driver appeared to take Her Majesty on her ride. We were surprised then when Her Majesty appeared with a lady in waiting and said, "Let's go I wish to go to the shrine of the Virgin to pray." I started to protest that I didn't know how to drive, when she said, "No arguments. You can drive and Diego will serve as guard." With that we found ourselves bodyguard and chauffeur for the Empress of Mexico. We drove the twenty minutes out to the shrine where the Empress alighted to pray. While she was praying I asked, "What do we do? It's just the two of us! What if something happens? I haven't fought for a long time and the two of us are no match for a gang." Quickly Diego replied "We will get her back to the palace as quick as possible. This time I'll drive and you'll be the bodyguard." He paused. "That way they'll try to kill you first."

We made it back to the palace and were quick to ask Schertzenlechner what to do. "I'll have the Sargent at Arms issue you each a firearm so you can protect their Imperial Majesties if need be," was his solution. As we walked back to our attic room Diego looked at me "I think I would rather have had the bell to answer."

Our new found responsibility continued the next day early when we heard a knock on the attic door. "Wake up," came the command from one of the footmen. "His Majesty wishes to take a ride in the country and Schertzenlechner says you two are his bodyguards for when he leaves early." I rolled out of bed and looked to see if I could make out any light to indicate that it was day. It was still pitch dark in our windowless room but even without a window I knew that we were up before dawn. "Come on. Let's go. It appears that we are now bodyguards when nobody else wants to be." We made it downstairs to the stables still rubbing our eyes and got the carriage ready. Just as we got the horse ready a maid came from the kitchen. "His Majesty just left his quarters and will be at the front door to the palace. Waste no time." We quickly holstered our firearms and Diego drove the coach to the front door while I held on firmly to the jump seat at the rear of the coach. We arrived at the front door just as it opened and Diego gave me a quick thumbs up with a smile. His Majesty appeared and said, "I want to head away from the capital and see what's out in the country." And with no further directions or waiting for company we set out for the country. Our ride took us several miles out in the country past the last house till it was just farm land and an occasional home. I had grown complacent sitting on the jump seat and, seeing nothing, my mind had started to wonder. Suddenly I was jarred to full attention when the Emperor cried out "What's that?" I pulled my firearm out of the holster faster than I thought possible when I saw the Emperor pointing at an old building. It looked like an old castle with a commanding view of the valley. "Pull in there," came the command. "I want to see it." We pulled up what looked like a driveway and discovered that the castle, if we could call it that, was empty. "I'm going to look around," he said. Realizing that we were responsible for the safety of the Emperor I took that as a command that we were to accompany him in the castle. Diego and I nodded at each other and, pulling out our weapons, went to the castle. We searched through the castle for nearly an hour looking through all the rooms and up to a balcony with a view across the valley. From there we climbed down and walked the grounds. Finally the Emperor said,

"We shall go now. Remember this route. We will take it again."

We got back to the palace and I assume that we were late for both Eloin and Shertzenlechner were waiting at the door. I had noticed that they couldn't stand each other and at the palace they usually tried to stay away from each other, yet still be close to the Emperor to have the most influence. The Emperor jumped out of the carriage with a smile of triumph. "I've found where I want my castle!"

Indeed, he had found his castle, and no matter what anybody might politely suggest he was intent on moving his household to what we found out was Chapultepec. Every morning for the next several weeks Diego and I were up early and driving him as his bodyguards out to Chapultepec where we tramped around the property and he detailed his dream for the property. We quickly learned that we were his scribes. One morning when we went on the tour he said, "Did you tell Eloin what I wanted?" When we replied that we hadn't "You must. How else will he know?" I didn't want to suggest the obvious, and from then on we carried a notebook to show Eloin. His only response usually was a shrug and "where will he get the money?"

I was starting to get the idea that Eloin wasn't the only one worried about money. The Emperor seemed to enjoy spending money and I overheard long time employees talking about his spending habits in Austria and Italy. I didn't need to worry about it, since my small salary wasn't going to break him but I mentioned it to Diego one night when we were getting ready for bed with the comment "How will he pay back money to Europe if he keeps spending money here?" To my surprise Diego responded "Why should we pay back money to Europe. You have stolen from us for over 300 years!" I should have ignored the "You have stolen," because, obviously he didn't mean that I had stolen money. Instead, being tired, I replied with an angry "I haven't taken a damn thing from Mexico. In case you've forgotten I didn't want to come here and just so you remember it was me who got you this job." In a bitter voice came the quick reply, "Yes. Tell the Mexican how much you have done for him before you take more from him!" With that we were at each other. I had my hands around his neck pounding his head against the floor while he took his right hand and landed several blows to my left eye. We went at it for several minutes till we heard a door slam nearby and a voice call out "What's wrong?" We pulled off from each other but still were furious and continued to fight quietly "See what you did you bastard" he hissed. "You started it" I muttered right back. "Look what you did you SOB! I think my nose is broken." Both of us had nosebleeds and the back of Diego's head was bleeding from where I had pounded it against the floor. We sat glaring at each other and breathing heavily for several minutes. Our fists were clenched and arms ready to land another punch and each was willing the other to start the fight again but not wanting to throw the first blow. We both knew the fight wasn't over but we both knew we couldn't fight anymore in our upstairs room without upsetting the house and our jobs.

We woke early the next morning to take the Emperor on his trip and didn't say a word to each other while we prepared the carriage. Without saying a word I jumped in the driver's seat determined to be in charge for the day. Diego said nothing, but climbed in the jump seat with cap pulled low over his eyes. Meeting us at the front door was the Emperor and Schertzenlechner. The Emperor took one look at me and said, "Good God. Who did this to you?" Sensing Diego's eyes on me I just said, "Your Majesty I ran into a door." "Well, I hope the door looks as bad as you," came the reply. "Off to Chapultepec. Schertzenlechner I want to show you my plans." And off we went.

When we arrived at Chapultepec His Majesty said, "We will be fine. No need to come with us. Stay here with the carriage. I think you and the door have things to discus." and they left, Maximilian clutching plans in hand. We said nothing for several minutes till Diego said, "He's right. We have things to discus," and he began talking.

"I don't think you understand how we Mexicans feel about being controlled by another country." I started to object but he cut me off, "No. Listen for now. I told you that my grandfather Diego is a legend in my family. What I haven't told you is that he was best friends with a Spaniard and together they witnessed the first battle for freedom." I must have looked surprised, "Yes." He continued. "Grandpa Diego, whom I'm named for, was friends with a Spanish boy and they were in Dolores when Father Hidalgo called for freedom from Spain." I remembered others talking about Father Hidalgo ringing the church bell in the middle of the night and gathering together an army to fight the Spaniards. "Grandpa Diego and his friend Rodrigo then went back to Guanajuato with my great grandfather. They were best friends despite their differences." With that I started to feel guilty and a lump came to my throat. "Great grandfather Jose knew that Rodrigo and his family were in danger and went to Rodrigo's home and encouraged them to hide with them because he knew that war was coming to Guanajuato." I felt a tear coming unbidden to my eye. I had heard the story before that an army of thousands had marched into the city and killed hundreds of Spaniards. "Rodrigo's father at first refused to hide with them. He was sure that the Alhondiga warehouse would be safe for all the Spaniards. Jose knew better and at the last minute with the army entering the city he and grandpa ran to Rodrigo's house and persuaded them to hide with them. They left the back door of Rodrigo's house as the army was breaking down the front door. They tried to run back to Grandpa's house but Grandpa Diego and Rodrigo got separated from the others and in the crush of the advancing army took refuge in a building across the street from the Alhondiga. They witnessed the battle first hand. They saw people being killed, and then when it was over they were caught by Hidalgo. Grandpa thinks it was only because Hidalgo was overcome by the battle too that he didn't order Rodrigo killed and him thrown in jail. Instead they were released and told to find their families. Grandpa said it was so terrible that blood was flowing in the streets." I thought how hard that must have been to witness and then Diego continued. "Do you see the desperation that these people felt to kill so many people that blood would flow through the streets? Do you understand what freedom means to a people willing to kill like that?" Then with tears coming to his eyes, "Grandfather was best friends with a Spaniard and risked his life to help his family survive. I don't want to see more war and I don't want to see my friends killed, but we must have freedom." With that the tears that had been forming in my eyes burst forth. "I'm sorry." I said. "I didn't understand what it means to you and what it means to others. I'm sorry. Will you forgive me?" "Yes," came the immediate reply. "I want to have a friend like Grandpa Diego did. You are that friend. We had better quit crying now. Here comes the Emperor and Schertzenlechner. We don't want to have to explain why we are crying. I'll tell you the rest of the story later. They all risked their lives again. I hope we don't have to do that."

We quickly changed places and Diego sat in the driver's seat while I moved to the jump seat still drying my tears as the Emperor approached. If he noticed anything he didn't say anything only "There! That's what I want the castle to look like. Find the money." From the driver's seat I'm sure that Diego was smiling as he made a clicking sound to start the horses back to the palace. Upon arriving at the palace we spent the morning working in silence in the stables. This time it was a companionable silence.

"We shall be moving the royal household to Chapultepec starting next week" announced the Emperor with the finality of Divine Right. "Thank you in advance for all the work to make this happen." Although Diego and I knew it was coming since we had been driving with the Emperor on a daily basis it was a surprise for others in the household. "What's out there?" a footman asked me. "Is it safe?" asked another. Not really feeling like I could answer I just said, "It's a large castle with a beautiful view. I think we will be happy there." What I didn't add was "once it gets repaired," for in truth just as the palace was starting to feel at home we would be moving to another castle in disrepair. I wondered to myself if the Emperor had any idea how much all of this would cost.

We would not know for almost as soon as he announced the move he was gone. We had gotten up early to get the carriage ready for him to visit Chapultepec and just as we arrived at the stables we saw soldiers riding horses leaving the stable and in the midst of them was the tall Emperor. "Where are they going?" I asked one of the stablehands. "I heard them talk about visiting the North." He replied. "I don't know. I just get the horses ready." Diego looked longingly at the horses as they disappeared from view. "I wonder if he's going to Guanajuato?" He thought out loud. "It's to the North." We discovered later that Charlotte was going to go with him but plans changed and so he left on horseback. With the Emperor gone the Empress was left in charge as regent. She held daily meetings with General Bazaine, government officials, and royal staff. I overheard one official say as he left a meeting, "She leads the meeting and by gosh things are accomplished. Not like…" and then he stopped and put his hand over his mouth, afraid that somebody was listening. The news filtering back was that the Emperor had gone to Guanajuato, Queretaro, Irapauto, and Celaya. All cities to the north of Mexico City but considered the center of Mexico. "Oh if I would have known maybe I could have gone with him to Guanajuato," sighed Diego as we worked taking more belongings on the several mile trip from the National Palace to Chapultepec. "He left with only soldiers." I replied. "You know you wouldn't have been able to keep up on horse with the soldiers." "You're right." He replied. "Maybe if I practice riding on the way back to the palace?" From then on we brought another horse with us when we left the palace, using the excuse that we might not have enough room on the wagon. The stablehands didn't seem to mind and as long as the Empress or Eloin, who had stayed here, didn't see us we were happy. The first day Diego was able to saddle the horse, although the stablehands did laugh when on his first attempt he put the saddle on backwards. Diego laughed too once he realized what he had done. With some kidding from the stablehands he was able to put his foot in the stirrup and climb up to sit on the saddle. "This is taller than the mules." The horse, sensing an inexperienced rider, kicked and bucked and Diego was thrown to the manure much to the laughter of the stablehands and myself. He got up laughing and while brushing the manure off his clothes asked "Is that the wild horse you give to new riders?" The stablehands didn't confess to that but one did bring out another horse. "Here. Here's 'Flora,' we use her with the children. Maybe she won't buck you off." Flora turned out to be just about right as Diego and I learned how to ride. It would be a long time before we could try 'Firebolt,' as we discovered the name of the first horse.

For the next several weeks we practiced riding with Flora on our daily trips to Chapultepec. As we got better the stablehands tried us with another horse that was a little more spirited. "Fuego," or "Fire," was a spirited deep brown horse and when the sun shone on her mane it almost looked like fire. She was spirited but the stablehands told us she would do anything for a little sweet. We took to swinging by the kitchen and stealing a sugar cube each morning and Fuego was ours to command.

With the Emperor gone and the household moving to Chapultepec we had time to talk as we went back and forth between the palace and the new castle. "You told me about your grandpa and the battle. What happened next?" I asked as we were heading back to the palace one afternoon, me riding Fuego beside the wagon Diego was driving. "I said that they risked their lives again. Actually they risked their lives more than once after the taking of the Alhondiga which is what they called the battle in Guanajuato. Rodrigo's family was hiding in grandpa and great grandpa's house. They couldn't be seen or the rebels would have killed Rodrigo and his family. Grandpa and great grandpa could have been jailed for harboring Spaniards." I questioned "Or worse?" "Yes. I think they could have been killed too. Anyway, grandpa and Rodrigo decided that they wanted to see if anything was left in Rodrigo's house and so they waited until everybody was asleep and snuck out of the house. They went through the dark streets to Rodrigo's house in the center of Guanajuato. When I was little grandpa loved to point out the window that they crawled through at the back of the house." "It's still there?" I asked. "Yes. Everything is still there. My grandpa loved taking me to all the places and pointing out what he did when he was little. Then he would tell me to never do what he had done because it was dangerous. Then he would always say, 'You do anything to help your friends.'" I laughed at the contradictions. "So they climbed in the back window and searched the whole house to see if anything was left. Just as they were leaving they got caught by a man in the house. Grandpa thought they would be killed and the man was dragging them through the house and suddenly there was some thunder that startled the man and they were able to get loose and escape through the window." I laughed again this time with Diego. "Both of them got whipped when they got home but grandpa said it was worth it for all the times he's told the story over the years." "What happened to Rodrigo?" I asked. "Oh grandpa and Rodrigo had to steal donkeys and weapons for Rodrigo's family to escape. They went out again at night, but this time with permission, and hid themselves in the Alhondiga before the soldiers locked it up for the night. Then after all the guards were asleep they snuck in to a storage room and stole some weapons and knives. I guess the hardest part of the night was opening the door of the Alhondiga when they left without anybody hearing." I was fascinated at the daring of Diego's grandfather. "Where did they get the donkeys?" "They went down the street to where some donkeys were stabled and walked right in to the stables in the middle of the night and took two donkeys and let the others out so that people would think the donkeys had escaped on their own. Grandpa always laughs when he tells that story because the donkeys just walked around Guanajuato and nobody knew what had happened!" We laughed together at the idea of donkeys just walking through the town. "Do you suppose we will have adventures like that?" I asked. "I can tell about being thrown from 'Firebolt.' You can tell about dining with the Empress." We laughed the rest of the way back to the palace.

By now it had been over a month that the Emperor was gone. Charlotte was keeping busy as regent and the move to the Chapultepec was nearly finished. We spent our first night in Chapultepec trading one attic room for another. "At least this attic has a window." I said. "And it's closer to the kitchen." Diego added. Word came that Maximilian would be returning soon and Charlotte made plans to meet him outside the city. It was not going to be just a short trip to the train station, but a caravan to meet him. We put together a caravan of wagons and carriages to travel all day and spend the night. A tent was set up for Charlotte and others for the dignitaries. Diego and I slept in the open and fortunately it did not rain.

The next morning a rider came and informed us that the Emperor was on his way and Charlotte went out to meet him riding Thunderbolt. When I saw which horse she was riding I poked Diego and said, "She rides better than you on Thunderbolt!" Diego just smiled but soon I felt dried manure thrown against my back. When I turned around all I saw was Diego's back diligently at work taking down one of the tents.

Charlotte was gone part of the morning and when the sun was midway in the sky we saw her returning with an escort of soldiers led by Bazaine. Each soldier was wearing the red, blue, and white uniform of the French army and each one held their sword high in a show of respect. In the midst rode the Emperor with a smile on his face. They paused for a few minutes while we readied the horses to return. I heard the Emperor saying, "Yes. It was a wonderful trip. The crowds were cheering for the Empire when I led the 'Grito' in Dolores. I did get sick in Queretaro, and thought only of you. The next time you must come too. The people want to see their Empress." I glanced over at Diego who was attaching the bridle to one of the wagon horses and could nearly read his thoughts about a foreigner leading the 'Grito.' I didn't have time to ask him as Maximilian and Charlotte continued on the trail back to Chapultepec and, with a creak of the wagon wheels, we followed.

That evening there was a celebration at Chapulepec. The Emperor had returned and ordered a fiesta. Each staff member was given beer, and tequila was passed around surreptitiously by some of the men. The Emperor walked around and greeted each person and thanked them for the help in moving to Chapultepec. When he got to us he said, "Well boys, I understand your riding skills are improving. Good! I will need both of you to ride with me as guards when I take my morning ride. Thunderbolt is waiting!" And with that he left to talk with the next person. Diego looked up at me and before I could say anything said, "You're taking Thunderbolt. I've got Flora."

And so began the new normal. His Majesty would get up early and take his ride at 5:00 AM. We would ride at a short distance allowing him the privacy he wanted, but close enough in case he needed something. "I don't exactly feel like I would be much good." Diego said once as we watched him race ahead of us. "He can ride much faster than either of us, and I don't think I could aim this pistol and ride at the same time." I had to agree. Although Firebolt now tolerated us, we hadn't really mastered him yet and there was usually a discussion about who would get Flora. As far as using the pistols we had been issued I just hoped we wouldn't have to use them.

After the Emperor returned from his ride he would take his breakfast with the Empress and do some work at Chapultepec. Then sometime in the morning he would take the carriage with soldiers accompanying him and go to the palace. The road that was now well used between the castle and the palace he decreed would be called "Avenida Carlota," for the Empress.

Although there was a routine to our lives now I still felt an undercurrent of danger. Bandits or rebels had destroyed the telegraph line between Mexico City and Vera Cruz. Although Mexico City was safe there were raids or attacks along the outskirts. General Bazaine did not appear worried. I heard him say to the Empress as he was leaving one day, "These things will sort themselves out. The rebels are on the run."

I didn't share his optimism. I really had no options except to stay in the employ of the Emperor. On my meager salary I couldn't afford to take a ship to Rome. As far as working my way across the ocean as I did getting here, Vera Cruz might as well be the other side of the world. No. I was stuck in Mexico and if I was stuck I should only hope for peace.

One day we were on our usual 5:00 AM ride trailing the Emperor by about 50 yards. It had been a pleasant morning and the rainy season was giving way to cooler mornings and comfortable afternoons. We were riding through the fields about a thirty minute ride from the castle and the Emperor was on a trail that meandered briefly into a thicket of trees and then out again to the fields. We had ridden through there before and I had suggested it would be a nice place to take a lunch and sit in the shade during the summer. Suddenly from behind a tree that the Emperor had just passed stepped a man with a lasso. The Emperor didn't see him because he had been hiding in the thicket away from the trail. The man couldn't see us riding behind because he had been hiding behind the tree. For all the man knew, the Emperor was traveling alone. We watched in horror as the man, with his eyes on the back of the Emperor began twirling the lasso. I shouted "Sire!" at the same time he threw the lasso and shouted "Down with the Emperor! Death to the invaders!" Distracted by my shout, the man, I shall call him a bandit, let the rope fall too soon and the loop, instead of snagging the Emperor fell harmlessly to the ground. Not to be deterred, the man pulled a knife from his jacket and went lunging toward the Emperor. Diego and I each pulled our pistols from the holsters and started to aim. We both realized at the same time that we would never be able to hit the man without hitting or possibly killing the Emperor. With a roar I threw my pistol to the ground, leapt from Firebolt (having lost the discussion) and tackled the man. The man turned as we both fell to the ground, his knife arm pulling back as if to stab me as I used my running start against him. Once on the ground I was trying to hit his face with my right hand while protecting my body and grabbing his knife arm with my left hand. The man struggled under my body and nearly freed his knife arm from my grip when I saw a flash go by my head and land squarely on the head of the attacker. I looked up and Diego was holding a stone that hit the now unconscious attacker. Diego was shouting "No. There are…" and then he paused as if thinking better of his words and said, "No. There are soldiers coming to take you." His Majesty looked shaken and took the lasso and between the three of us tied him up. "Thank you boys," He said while we tied him up. "You saved my life and I am grateful. The Empress will be too and you shall be rewarded." Looking at me he said, "Did you think anything like this would happen when you jumped on board the ship?" I was in favor of waking up the attacker and making him run behind us while we went back to the castle. Diego pointed out that we were a thirty minute ride away from the castle and it would probably take an hour if we forced him to run behind us. In the end we made a check of the area for more bandits while Maximilian stayed with the tied up bandit. Deciding that the attacker acted by himself we hoisted him to Flora so that his legs were on one side of the horse while his head the other. Diego and I shared Firebolt while the Emperor led the way back to the castle. It might have been faster to have him walk, since we had to stop several times and adjust him on the back of the horse. By the time we got back to the castle he was starting to come to. By the time we entered the gates he was swearing and shouting "Down with the Emperor. Death to the invaders!" With those shouts the compound woke. Soldiers came running from the barracks and doors opened to see what was happening. The soldiers surrounded the man and pulled him away. His Majesty shouted, "Treat him kindly. We must not repay evil with evil." I don't know how the French soldiers planned on treating him but I don't think they paid much attention to what the Emperor was saying. With all the commotion in the courtyard Charlotte was woken from sleep in her chambers. She came out, pale in face, "What happened my Lord?" using a formal term to address him. "Oh just an unhappy man. The boys here saved me. Boys! No. These aren't boys. They are men who risked their lives to protect me. I think the Order of Guadalupe is necessary." The Order of the Virgin of Guadalupe is one of the royal awards that Maximilian created on his trip across the ocean. I remember them talking about the award when I was serving dinner once. With that he turned and without another word disappeared into the castle.

Suddenly with all the excitement of the morning I felt weak in the knees and sat on the ground. One of the stablehands came and took away Flora and Firebolt while Diego and I sat in silence for a few minutes. "Well." He said. "I guess we had our danger. What will we tell our grandchildren?" Remembering then that it looked like he pulled back words when he said, "The soldiers are coming." I asked, "Were you going to say something else? You know there were no soldiers coming." With a sheepish look he said, "I started to say, 'There are other ways to end the Empire.' Please believe me. I don't want to kill the Emperor. I just think that Mexicans need to solve their problems and it should be done without killing." I thought for a moment. "You know. I think your grandfather would be proud of you." We said nothing more about the incident and went to the kitchen for breakfast.

By the end of the day word had spread throughout the castle. Schertzenlechner and Eloin put aside their animosity for a few moments and came together to congratulate and thank us. "You boys did a good job and the Empire thanks you." Eloin said, somewhat sanctimoniously, forgetting that the Emperor had called us 'men.' Schertenlechner pulled some coins from his pocket. "Here." He said. "I think you deserve this." And handed each of us several coins. We thanked them and I said, "We were just doing our duty." And they left. I looked at Diego and said, "I don't think we are going to get the Order of Guadalupe."

After a couple of days things began to settle down. We received congratulations for several days and the Empress sent us each a letter of thanks. Perhaps the best thing to happen was that the General decided that the Emperor's morning rides around Chapultepec now required more security than two teen age boys and we were replaced by soldiers of the French army. One of the officers, Lieutenant Lopez came to tell us that our services would no longer be required to guard the Emperor on his daily rides, "This is not a reflection on your service. Indeed the Emperor, Empress, and General Bazaine are most appreciative of your service. The General has decided that the Emperor's morning rides require more security." He continued as if we were offended that we no longer were required to get up at 5:00 AM. "Now if you will hand over the pistols you were assigned we can be done here." We willingly handed over the pistols and Diego said, "I don't think I ever could have shot it at a target." Lieutenant Lopez asked "Didn't you have shooting lessons before you were given the pistols?" I told him the story about how the Empress quickly needed a driver, "And so they gave us pistols when we took the Empress on her ride and then the Emperor just continued with us." Diego added, "I didn't try to use the weapon when the Emperor was under attack because I was sure that I would shoot him or Leo by accident, so I saw the rock and knocked the man on the head." Lopez stared at us for a moment. "Well. Good thinking on both your parts. I shall tell the Emperor that you need shooting lessons. We need quick thinkers around here." And so, although we no longer had to get up early to go with the Emperor on his rides, the time was now taken up with shooting lessons. Lieutenant Lopez took it on himself to call for us the next morning saying, "The Emperor has approved your lessons. You are to train with some of the soldiers on the shooting range every morning." He took us to another officer and said, "See to it that these men are issued weapons after they have completed lessons." The shooting range was located in the fields away from the castle so that the sound did not interfere with the work of the castle. Our mornings now consisted of learning how to use the weapons of the French army. "I hope I never have to use this," said Diego one morning, "but I suppose it's a good thing to know." Indeed, it was good to talk with the soldiers. They told us what was going on with the war against the rebels and what they had heard about the politics of Mexico in France. "Napoleon is under pressure to get out of Mexico," said one solder. "I got a letter from home saying so." Another soldier said that Juarez was on the move and cities that had once declared for the Empire were now part of rebel territory. "As soon as we leave a city the rebels will come back and the people will declare for the republic. This whole 'Mexico Adventure' is going to end poorly for France." He concluded. A third soldier, listening in on the conversation said, "Learn how to use the weapons. You might need them to save your lives."

STRUGGLES

We were in our attic room one night after having started the day at 5:00 with shooting practice and working all morning at Chapultepec. The brief siesta we had after lunch was followed by work all afternoon and evening at the National Palace at one of Her Majesty's many dinners. "I'm dead tired." I said. "And we have to start it all over again tomorrow." Diego laughed, but then turned serious. "Do you suppose that the soldiers are right? Do you think the Empire is losing?" I thought for a moment. "It doesn't look good for him. That's for sure. I suppose it's good that we are learning to shoot." "I suppose so. I sure would like to get back to Guanajuato, but I can't go till it's safe." He dropped in bed. "I'm dead. Good night." Soon I heard his steady breathing and I was left wondering if I would ever see home again.

The next morning at shooting practice one of the soldiers pulled us aside. "Watch your back." He said. "The Emperor has pardoned the man who tried to kill him. He's out of the cell where we had placed him. We thought he should be executed for trying to kill the Emperor, but the Emperor wants to show mercy in the hopes that the country will turn around." When we expressed surprise he continued. "People will see Maximilian as a nice man, but a weak ruler. Watch your back. That man will think of you as the reason he was in jail and try to kill you next time." These soldiers had become our protectors and another said, "Keep practicing. You don't want to be like the Belgian soldiers!" Diego questioned. "What happened? I knew that some soldiers from Belgium had come to Mexico." He spat. "They weren't given enough training and sent out to Michoacan to fight. They were surrounded by rebels and killed. The Empress is angry and blames the General. She regards the Belgians as her soldiers and treats them like family." The first soldier continued, "The Empire forces Mexican men to be soldiers who might otherwise be soldiers for Juarez. As soon as they can desert they do. Sometimes they take their weapons with them and take up arms against us. If they are caught the Emperor just pardons them and there's nothing we can do. If I could get out of here and go home I would." I thought the same thing.

A few weeks later we were summoned early before shooting practice. "You're needed at the palace immediately." Came the voice at the door to our attic room. "Well, I didn't want to practice today anyway," said Diego as he rolled over once in bed. We got ready and discovered that His Majesty hadn't even gone for his morning ride but had left already with a contingent of soldiers. "Quick. Get the other carriage ready for Her Majesty. She'll be going soon." I couldn't figure out what was so important that both His Majesty and the Empress left the castle so early. We got the carriage ready, and waited for the soldier guards to accompany us. "There are no soldiers left," said the quartermaster, handing us each a pistol, "you'll be the guards again." We must have looked surprised because he said, "Well. You have become proficient at shooting now. Lieutenant Lopez says you are back on guard duty." We didn't have time to question him as the Empress arrived and said, "Let's be on our way. The nuncio will arrive shortly." I assumed the position on the jump seat of the carriage while Diego drove. I wondered what a 'nuncio' was, and why he was causing so much trouble. We hadn't even gotten to the courtyard of the palace when a runner came out, "Your Majesty. His Majesty says that the nuncio will arrive at the train station and we should send a carriage." Her Majesty didn't even pause but said, "Quick. Stop. Let me off and dash to the railroad station to get the nuncio." I must have looked confused, but Diego only said, "Yes, Your Majesty. We will be back with him as soon as he arrives." Diego and I took off as fast as he could drive to the train station. "What's a nuncio?" I asked. If Diego was surprised he didn't show it. "The Papal Nuncio is the personal representative of the Holy Father to a region or country. The Holy Father has sent him to persuade His Majesty to change the law that Juarez made." I was confused. "What law did Juarez make?" Diego explained, "When Juarez came to power he pushed through a law that said that the Church and priests could not own property and confiscated all the property and sold it. The pope and the priests want the property back and so the nuncio is here to ask for it." I thought for a moment. "His Majesty won't like that." "No," came the reply. "Keep your ears open." We arrived at the train station just as a train pulled in to the station. I stayed with the carriage while Diego went in search for the Nuncio. He came back within a few minutes accompanied by a short, stocky priest who said nothing but jumped in the carriage. We returned quickly to the palace and presented him to the guards in front for admittance to Their Majesties. We brought the carriage around to the back courtyard and made the horses comfortable. We didn't know what else to do so decided to wait near the royal offices. We didn't wait too long. I could hear voices inside the offices, but couldn't make out words. Suddenly with a swish, the door opened and the Nuncio appeared at the door and left without saying a word. We hadn't been told to prepare a carriage for him so he must have been planning to stay in the palace. Suddenly the Empress and Bazaine appeared at the door too. "Well General. That did not go well. There is only one solution. We must throw him out the window." I'll admit that the Empress had a wicked sense of humor.

The troubles around the palace continued. I should say that the Palace was first the palace and seat of government. His Majesty still went there daily from the Castle which was now his home. Once I was sent to the palace from Chapultepec with messages from Her Majesty. I went riding Thunderbolt, proud that I had finally accomplished riding this horse. When I arrived I told the guards that I had a message from the Empress. To my amazement I was sent right up to his offices and when I arrived in the outer office I saw Schertzenlechner just starting to enter the office. He looked at me and questioned "Is there a problem at the castle?" I replied that I had message for His Majesty. "Well. Does it need a reply?" "Yes. Her Majesty is expecting a reply." Hearing the conversation the Emperor called out, "Come in." I bowed quickly and said, "Your Majesty. A message from Her Majesty, the Empress," and handed over the sealed envelope. He had barely opened the envelope when Eloin rushed in to the room and shouted "You liar!" at Schertzenlechner while grabbing him by the lapels of his jacket and pushing him around the room. I was surprised and wanted to leave, but by then both of them in their fight had blocked the door. It was common knowledge in court that the two could not stand each other, but this was the first time I had seen the hatred erupt so openly. Their words got louder and louder and again I tried to leave but they kept circling around and I finally stepped back and tried to pretend I didn't hear anything. In the roar I did hear Eloin say loudly, "You're just a butler! Your Majesty, he is still receiving his salary as a butler from the Austrian Court as well as a salary from you!" If this was a surprise to the Emperor he didn't show it. He sat at his desk with a tired look on his face. One that I'm sure I saw on my father's face when he was disappointed in me. The argument reached a new high with the last accusation, which Schertzenlechner did not deny. Instead he tried a new tack. "You can't run this government without me." He shouted. "I have the support of the Mexicans! You," He shouted at Eloin, "are just a geologist sent by Belgium! You only want to become rich at the expense of the Mexicans!" The argument got louder and I felt embarrassed for the Emperor. Finally Schertzenlechner shouted in what I assume was a bluff "You'll never be able to govern without me. I quit! I resign!" The Emperor looked up from his desk and said the obvious, "I accept your resignation." Schertzenlecher looked shocked as his bluff was called, and turned to leave slamming the door so hard that the walls shook and two paintings fell. His Majesty looked up from the desk at Eloin and said, "Now. Where were we? Oh Yes. Leo. You have a message from Her Majesty that needs a reply."

The court soon lit up with the news of Schertzenlechner's departure. People were sure that he shouted out his resignation in the belief that the Emperor would beg him to reconsider. The stories of his words and actions that day ranged from a simple "I quit," to threats against Eloin and His Majesty. I didn't add to any of these stories. At first I couldn't wait to get back to the castle to tell Diego and then I remembered what Georg had said about not spreading rumors so I didn't even tell people that I had been in the room when it had happened. I realized that if word did get out about what had happened that His Majesty knew exactly who was in the room and, being the youngest and least important, I knew that I could be easily blamed for the leak. When Diego finally heard about it he asked me if I knew anything about the rumors. With a silent prayer asking forgiveness for lying I said, "No. I don't know what happened." I vowed someday to tell him, but for now I couldn't.

GUANAJUATO

Letter to home:

My dear Father and Maria.

It has now been over a year that I have been here. I find myself happy here. I have grown and matured. I hope that if you were to see me that you would agree. I have been kept busy in the employ of the Emperor of Mexico. Sometimes I drive the carriage that he uses between his residence and the National Palace where his offices are. I think about coming back to Europe, but, but am happy and busy here for now. Things are not all work though. Last week we celebrated the wedding of General Bazaine to a Mexican woman Pepita de la Pena. I'll tell you that my friend Diego and I were there when they met. We were pressed into service at the last minute to help at a Ball and that is where General Bazaine met Pepita. He went right up to her and said, "Excuse me, but you remind me of my wife who has been gone for a year." We were surprised at how forward he was but it seems to have worked. The wedding was very nice and we servants were all invited to be in the background at the reception to offer congratulations. I do not know if General Bazaine will stay in Mexico or go back to France.

Now as for the news that you might hear over there. Do not worry. I am fine and happy. The Emperor is in control and the rebels are on the run. I'm sure whatever you hear is exaggerated so please don't worry. Please be sure of my love and that I send you my best wishes.

Your son,

Leopold

Most of what I wrote was true. I did think about going back to Europe but had no money. The wedding was true, and it had been a grand affair. I really was not sure about the rebels being on the run. I think, in my heart, I believed that they were on the run toward Mexico City and control of the country. But I was happy and really had no plans on leaving.

Bad news continued. Charlotte's father, the king of the Belgians, died and the court went in mourning. Black fabric or paper was everywhere in the city. We servants were all given black armbands to wear as a sign of mourning.

News came from the United States that the North had won. This news set the court on edge. With their Civil War over the United States might have more time to interfere in Mexico and the Americans wouldn't look favorably on an Emperor in their back yard. Then the news went from bad to worse within a couple weeks when we found out that Abraham Lincoln, their president, had been assassinated. Maximilian sent a letter to the new US president offering his condolences. The rumor was that it was returned unopened as the United States would not recognize Maximilian as Emperor of Mexico.

Then some news came that made Diego nearly dance for joy and sent me into a deep depression. "The Emperor and Empress will take a tour of the realm to the North. The cities will include Queretaro, Guanajuato, and San Luis Potosi." announced Eloin, the new chief of staff since the departure of Schertzenlechner. "Guanajuato" breathed Diego. "I can go home! Even if they tell me I can't go I'll resign and follow the caravan to Guanajuato. I can finally go home." I could not share his joy at leaving. I felt at a loss. Diego had become my brother. Diego had become my family in the absence of my real family. His being so excited just made me that much more depressed.

Of course, Eloin couldn't just announce that we were going and it would happen. It took weeks of planning and preparation. Diego was nearly giddy with excitement and finally I could handle it no more. "You're acting like a little girl excited about a dance." I said, with some malice in my voice. Diego took offense. "Why are you so mad? Don't you understand? I haven't seen my family in years." "You!" I shouted. "Aren't the only one who hasn't seen his family." Diego looked as if he wanted to fight me again, and then came the realization "You're right. I'm sorry. You're far from your family too, and it must hurt to see me happy. You know you'll always be my brother. Why don't you leave service in Guanajuato too? You can find something to do." That stopped me dead and I thought, "Should I give up on going back to Europe? What do I have there? What do I have here? Is life in Imperial service a life?" I couldn't make up my mind and spent a sleepless night. I dreamed of the Empress shouting, "Bring me a chicken! Bring me a chicken!" while standing in a fountain again. I tossed and turned the whole night and only woke with Diego shaking me and telling me it was time to get to work.

The time till we left passed quickly. We had spent days packing equipment that the royal couple might need. Maids packed clothes and jewels to show the Mexicans that Maximilano and Carlota were here to stay. Everything must be done to present a strong and powerful Empire and Emperor. When Maximilian had gone before it was on a tour of inspection and he traveled with some aides and soldiers. Now things would be different. Now it was a state tour and everything must be done perfectly. Diego and I had officially been told that we would be traveling with the caravan as wagon drivers and bodyguards. Diego hadn't told anybody his intentions of leaving except for me. "I don't think anybody knows I'm from Guanajuato except for you. I won't ruin my chances by telling anybody."

Finally the day came to leave and we made a symbolic ride down Paseo de Carlota to the National Palace so the people of Mexico City could pay their respects to their Emperor. Our first stop of more than a night would be Queretaro. It would take us several days to get that far since the carriages and wagons couldn't go as fast as soldiers on horseback. In the meantime we drove the wagons and the soldiers on horseback kept at a slower pace to match our speed. In mid afternoon Lieutenant Lopez, as head of the caravan, called for us to stop for the day and set up guards. The Emperor and Empress went for a walk while Diego and I set up tents and the cook started preparations for our camp dinner.

We finished setting up tents and getting the Imperial Couple's personal effects set up in their tent in about an hour just as the sun was setting and the afternoon turning to twilight. Diego motioned down the trail, "Let's take a walk before it gets dark." Since we had set up camp near a stream we set off down the stream for a few minutes. We were chatting as we skipped stones, trying to keep each stone in the middle of the stream. Suddenly Diego grabbed my arm, "Look. What's that?" In front of us and to one side of the creek was a man. With a sinking heart I realized that he was the man who had tried to kill the Emperor. This time he was armed with a pistol and not a knife. Everything happened so quickly I didn't have time to react. He reached and grabbed Diego with one arm and put him in a headlock. With his other hand he took the pistol and placed it against Diego's head. "Don't try anything or your friend gets it." Then he saw who we were. "Ah. You! You ruined my plan to kill the invader once and now you've found me again. Well, if I can't kill him at least I'll be able to take my revenge on you." He smiled as he passed the pistol slowly up Diego's head from chin to forehead and down again. "Yes, I'll take my revenge on you." I was at a loss. Even though we both had the pistols we had been assigned they were useless with the man holding a pistol to Diego's head. I wouldn't be able to pull my pistol without him seeing it and shooting Diego. "Well well. What do we have here? The boys still have weapons. We will take care of that. You!" He growled, motioning his head at me. "Turn around and kneel. Don't try anything. I can shoot him." Knowing that I was stuck I did as I was told and knelt. "Now. With your fingers pull the pistol out of the holster and place it on the ground behind you." Since I had my back to him I couldn't tell if he was pointing the gun at me or Diego, but I slowly reached down and carefully pulled the gun out of its holster and tossed it underhanded backwards. "Good. Now. Face on the ground and hands above your head." I slowly lowered my hands to the ground and scraped them along the soil as I placed my face on the ground in front of me. There was a rustling sound and at first I thought that he was pulling the pistol to shoot me but I felt as Diego was roughly shoved face down at my side. "There. Maybe I can still kill the invader if I can get these two first." I saw my life flash before my eyes. Mother's death and Giovanni. I saw my hands reaching into Maria's bag to take money that I claimed as mine. I relived every harsh word to my father and regretted them all. "I wonder what death will feel like." I thought. I remembered the prayer on the Navarre where I asked God, "Can you fix this?" I supposed this was His answer. I had improved my life but it wasn't fixed. I was still far from home, about to become another statistic in Maximilian's Empire. My life continued to play before my eyes. I saw myself jumping aboard the ship and the sailor shouting "I lost a week's pay because of you," and then I saw myself shouting in a fight long ago, "I will not give up. I will survive!" Then I realized I still had a handful of soil in my hand from scraping it along the ground. Without thinking I rolled from my position and flung the soil at the man's face while shouting at Diego. "Move! Move! Move!" The man was surprised as the dirt got into his eyes and swore but managed to get a shot off in my direction. The bullet hit where I had just been and the man used his free hand to wipe the dirt from his eyes. It was all the time we needed as Diego rolled the opposite direction from me and we attacked from each side. We struggled and another shot rang out but we were able to overpower him in the rapidly growing dusk. I shouted, but the shots had already alerted the soldiers and soon we were surrounded and the man was roughly pulled away and we were safe. One of the soldiers who had become friendly with us swore. "It was the same man the Emperor pardoned. I was sure he would try something again" Lopez' face darkened. "That won't happen again." He pointed at the man and a couple soldiers. "Take him away. You know what to do." We were helped to our feet and through the brush back to the trail. As we got back to the trail we heard a volley of shots. Within a moment the soldiers came back empty handed. Lopez said nothing and we continued back to the camp. Once inside the camp he set additional soldiers on patrol. His Majesty looked up from dinner and said, "What happened Lopez? I thought I heard shots." Lopez replied. "It was nothing Your Majesty. Just soldiers getting some target practice in before dark." His Majesty smiled, "Good. It doesn't do any good for the soldiers to get rusty," and turned back to his meal.

Diego and I ate with the soldiers that evening. We sat around the fire and the soldiers asked us to tell everything that happened in detail. Diego told them how quickly everything happened and said. "We couldn't do a thing. It happened so fast." One of the older soldiers who looked like he had been through many battles said, "That's the way it goes, but you did quick thinking in throwing dirt in his face. Sometimes the simplest thing works. He won't bother us again and the Emperor won't have a chance to pardon him again. The vultures will eat him tonight." We sat silent for a long time staring at the fire. I was left to rethinking my words of the fight. "I will not give up. I will survive." Survival was getting harder and harder it seemed. I fell asleep by the fire and slept fitfully all night. "I will survive," kept ringing in my head.

The next morning we started pulling down the tents while the Emperor and Empress had their breakfast and soon we were on our way. "Well," said Diego from the wagon beside me. "I wonder what will happen today?"

The next two days were uneventful as we continued on to Queretaro. In Queretaro we were greeted by crowds cheering "Viva el Emperador" Again I felt proud to be part of this Empire even as an outsider. I noticed that Diego did not share my sentiments. When the crowds were cheering it seemed that he was always clenching his teeth as if willing himself not to say something. I thought about questioning him, but decided I knew his views.

From Queretaro we started the two night journey to Guanajuato. Diego seemed more and more excited with each step while I became more and more depressed. I tried to analyze my feelings, and I realized that I was mourning a loss. I was mourning the loss of a friendship of over a year. We had been through so much together and now it would be time to say goodbye. I wondered if he was thinking the same thing, despite his excitement at going home. As if sensing my thoughts he said, "You know I'm going to miss you and our work, but it is time for me to go home."

As we made the last leg of the journey from Irapauto I asked again about his grandfather and Rodrigo. "What happened after they stole the donkeys? Did they escape?" Diego replied. "We don't know. Grandfather says that they got all the supplies loaded on the donkeys and Rodrigo and his parents left Guanajuato early in the morning. They took the donkeys and the plan was to leave Guanajuato and make it to Mexico City and from there to Vera Cruz and back to Spain. They never heard of any battles between here and Mexico City so he thinks they might have made it." This story, that I had heard piecemeal for a year now ended without a clear ending. "That's no fair." I laughed.

"I want to know that everybody made it OK." Diego laughed too, "That's what I said when I was little whenever grandpa told the story. Maybe I thought that if I asked him to tell the story enough times the ending would change. He just always said that you do what you can for friends."

Finally we came to the city. It wasn't like a city that rose from the desert. It was a city that one looked down on before entering. Guanajuato is at the bottom of a valley and when we arrived at the top of the hill we could see across the valley to a church in the distance and at the bottom of the valley was the city, again, with churches filling the city. "Look." Said Diego. "In the distance there is the Alhondiga where grandpa and Rodrigo hid to steal the weapons. And this street here is the street that Hidalgo and his army used to come down into the city. From below they turned and went to the Alhondiga to take it." As we descended the hill into the city there were crowds cheering for the Emperor. "Listen." Diego had to shout over the roar of the crowd. "Guanajuato is full of people who have made their fortune from mining. These people will support the Empire." Indeed, it seemed as if the whole town had turned out to cheer the royal couple. We proceeded through the crowds and Maximilian and Carlota entered a building off the main square. Soon they appeared at a balcony on the third level of the building. Maximilian spoke a few words, but since we were sandwiched in behind everybody on the other side of the square we couldn't hear anything. "Come on!" Said Diego. "Let's go! I want to find my family! You can come with me! The Emperor won't need anything tonight, and the horses and wagons are all taken care of for now." I agreed that I could do that, hoping to put off as long as possible the moment when we would have to say goodbye.

We set off down the street where we had turned when we entered the city. "This street is called Sopeña. The street that we came down the hill and where Hidalgo entered is called 'Tecolote'" Diego continued in a rush, as if trying to impart all his wisdom in the few moments we had left. "And see here. Now we are on Campanero. That means 'bell,' remember. When a wagon came down the hill to enter the city somebody would come out and ring a bell, so that's why it's called that." I smiled at his excitement. "Here. This is Entendente Riaño's house. Grandpa was always afraid to walk down this street because he was afraid of the man. He was afraid of him until the night he actually met him and discovered he was pretty kind." Diego paused for a moment. "Riaño was one of the Spaniards killed at the Alhondiga. Grandpa saw him killed. Oh Grandpa will have so much to tell you. You'll like him." We started heading out of the main part of the town and Diego was nearly jumping for joy. "Now this part of the city is called 'Pastitas.' It's one of the older parts of the city, but not as old as the basilica of course." Diego was nearly dancing as we continued down the street. "We're getting closer now. It's been so long. My father still has the same carpentry shop that grandpa and great grandfather had. Look. There it is." He was pointing at a building with a large front door that looked like it could be opened to take in and out large pieces of furniture. Diego started running toward the shop. "Papa, Papa. It's me. I've returned." He shouted as he ran into the shop. Suddenly, stopping in bewilderment, he said, "Who are you? Where's my father?" I felt the world fall from under us.

LIFE GOES ON

We walked back to town, arms thrown over each other's shoulders. Diego hadn't said a word yet. I was stunned at what I had heard and I don't think Diego was comprehending it yet. The man behind the counter had looked at us in surprise, and then sorrow as he realized who Diego was. "Come here boy," he had said kindly. "They're gone. Dead. All of them. They were on their way to Leon and got caught in a skirmish between rebels and the French troops….There was no way to get in touch with you or find you. All we knew was that you had gone with your mother to visit family before all the problems. I've got the shop now." Diego had listened to the whole story without understanding. Finally he turned on his heels and we left the shop. We walked for over an hour, silent. I, trying to feel his pain, and he trying to comprehend what he had heard. "They're gone. He killed them" He said. I couldn't decide if it was a question or a statement. "Would you like to try and find the cemetery?" I questioned. "Would you like to pray at the cemetery?" "Pray." He spat. "What good would that do?" He allowed me to lead him across the city to where the man at the shop had said the bodies had been buried. We crossed in front of the building where the crowds were still calling for the royal couple. Had we just been there less than an hour ago? It now seemed like a lifetime.

We passed the Basilica and continued up the street to the cemetery. It was quiet here with most of the city still downtown cheering the Emperor. Diego stumbled around the stones for a few minute until he stopped, and without emotion said, "Here." I came over and saw the simple stone, "Gonzalez." Diego sat on the stone and tears flowed down his face. "I'm sorry Daddy. I'm sorry I wasn't here to be with you. I tried to get home." The words continued, unheard and unanswered. I sat a short distance away, sensing the need for private grief. We sat there for over two hours and, with the sun setting, I pulled Diego away from the graves. "Come. It's late. Let's go back." He let me lead him out of the cemetery without a word.

I took him back to downtown where the crowds were still thronged in front of the hotel where Maximilian was in residence. I hadn't thought about where we would sleep. Diego had planned on staying at home and I had just assumed I would stay with him until it was time to leave with the Emperor. Fortunately the soldiers who had adopted us as their own saw us. I quietly told them what had happened. "Here boy. Come with us. We are staying down the street. You Leo, stay with him. We'll have somebody else check on your chores for the evening." We backtracked up the street we had come from and turned right and went up the hill to a warehouse where the soldiers had set up camp. Diego looked up at the building and said, "The Alhondiga. This is were the first battle was." I looked at him and started to apologize. "I'm sorry I didn't know they were coming here. I can take you…" "No." He interrupted. "I want to tell the story again." And

so he told the story again about how the Spaniards under
the Intendente had chosen this building as their fort for
when the rebels attacked. They had gathered here behind
locked door and listened to the attack outside. "My
grandfather was in that building there." He said, pointing
across the street. "On the upper floor. He had hidden there
with his friend after they got separated from their
families." Diego paused and one of the soldiers prodded
him. "What happened next?" "Next." Diego laughed.
"They got caught by Hidalgo and his soldiers. They let
them go and told them to go find their families." He
laughed bitterly. "Families. They had families." There was
silence for several minute and Diego continued "Several
weeks later they slipped in through this door and hid up
there in that room and waited for the soldiers to fall asleep.
When everyone was asleep they broke into that room there
and stole some weapons." He laughed bitterly again.
"They thought they were caught when a soldier woke up
and started walking around the courtyard. He was just
using the outhouse." He finished Rodrigo's story and sat
there without a sound. The soldiers had pulled together
some blankets and we stretched out on the ground of the
first battle for Mexican independence. I don't think Diego
slept all night. I slept fitfully and dreamt of people
attacking the Alhondiga with firebrands.

I awoke the next morning with sunlight in my eyes. I
looked over and Diego was laying there with his eyes
open. "Did you sleep?" "No." He replied. "I was awake all

night trying to think what to do. I have no family here now, even though it's my birthplace. I could stay here but there wouldn't be much for me." I questioned "What other options do you have?" "I could try and return to Vera Cruz and live with my cousins there." "Or," I suggested. "you could continue working for the Emperor." I'll admit that I suggested that selfishly, but it was still an option. "Yes. That's true." He concluded. "I suppose that's best for now. There's nothing here for me. The shop isn't mine either and I wasn't trained to be a carpenter anyway. I will not run. I will survive. Where have I heard that before?" He asked with a sad smile. We left the Alhondiga and returned down the hill to the central part of the town. The Emperor and Empress had chosen to stay in town and receive visitors in their quarters and we were left with a free day. "I might as well show you the rest of the city. I think I'll feel better if I tell you the stories again." We had been standing in front of the hotel where the Emperor was and he pointed to the left. "Here. This way to Rodrigo's house." And we walked to the end of the courtyard and turned right and then left again to find ourselves in another plaza. "Here." He pointed to a large house taking up the whole front of the plaza. "This is Rodrigo's house, and here." He said, leading me through an alley and pointing. "Is the window that Grandpa would use to climb in and out to see Rodrigo. It's the same window that they used when they escaped from the drunk guard." He added with a laugh. "I've heard that story so many times I feel like it happened to me. It took fifty years, but an empire killed him" "You know." I said. "We are making our own stories: here and now." "Yes," came the reply. "It just hurts so." We left the plaza, that he told me was called 'Baratillo,' and continued through the town almost back to the Alhondiga. "Here. This is the stable where they stole the donkeys." And then pointing up the hill at the church on the hillside. "I've never told you how they got in trouble for hiding away in the wagon and going up to the church. There's no time to go up there today. Maybe another day."

We worked our way back to the center stopping to have something to eat in front of the hotel where the royal couple was staying. "Do you think he will win?" asked Diego. "Who?" I asked, momentarily surprised. "Maximilian? I don't know. It looks difficult now. Doesn't it? With the Americans not at war it might force France to leave." Diego looked at me for a moment. "I suppose I might as well work for the Emperor as long as there is one." Then he added cryptically "Then maybe I can find a way to…" But he didn't finish.

We returned to the Alhondiga and prepared to bed down for the night. I was looking forward to a good night sleep since I had slept so little the night before. The soldiers had built a fire to take the edge off the evening chill. "Come on boys. Sit down and share some cheer." One said, pulling out a bottle of tequila. We went over and he offered each of us a swig. "We are celebrating. The rumor is that Napoleon will pull us home," said one. "Of course it's just a rumor, but it's as good a reason as any to celebrate" said another. "Do you think that will happen?" I asked. Lopez, hearing the discussion, came over. "Don't start expecting things to happen soon." He said. "That's the quickest way to be buried here." We chuckled and went to the spot where we had slept the night before. Lopez followed. "Watch yourselves wherever you are. Things are not what they look. Make sure you take care of yourself." We agreed and soon were sound asleep with the sounds of the city fading to silence.

The next day marked the start of the journey back to Mexico City. It would take several days and we would stay in Queretaro again but I hoped the journey would help Diego work through his grief. We were driving one of the wagons loaded with supplies for an imperial journey. Diego sat and stared straight ahead for most of the first day and wouldn't talk. If I tried to ask questions I would get a monosyllabic grunt or a quick reply. This continued for two more days, and finally the morning of the third day he woke with a smile on his face. "Things will be ok." He announced. "Like you said, 'I will survive. I will not run.' I'm going to be ok." I was going to question his change in attitude, but was so happy to see my friend back to normal I couldn't.

The arrival back in Mexico City was marked by cheering crowds and a parade down Paseo de Carlota from the National Palace to Chapultepec. It felt good to be 'home,' at least to this routine. Rome was starting to feel far away in my heart and I wondered if it would ever feel like 'home' again. Indeed I wondered if Mexico was home. The next day the word came down that the rumors we had been hearing were true. Maximilian had received a letter from Napoleon saying that the French troops would be removed over the next 18 months leaving the Empire with only Mexican troops. Both the Emperor and Empress when they were seen by the staff looked as if they had been betrayed. Diego looked thrilled. I didn't know how I felt.

We hardly had a chance to be back at Chapultepec before we were off again. This time it was Maximilian himself off to Cuernavaca. He had bought an estate there and used it as a retreat from Chapultepec. "Retreat." One of the soldiers had sniffed. "He's hiding from the war and spending Napoleon's money to boot. He's also spending time with a …" but stopped before saying who or what he was spending time with.

Cuernavaca was a full day's journey from Chapultepec and this time Diego and I were sent as bodyguards and aides during the trip. I had never really felt like a bodyguard, but this time Lieutenant Lopez and soldiers rode with us, so we acted more as aides than anything else. We had never been there before and I was eager to see what about it had drawn the Emperor away from Chapultepec. We didn't have long to wait. As we descended the mountains toward the more tropical Cuernavaca it seemed that the Emperor's personality changed. In Mexico City he was more formal. Here, away from Charlotte and the palace he was more open with the elites he brought with them. Over dinner that Diego and I served his jokes with the others became more earthy. As the evening went on and the stories became more and more explicit I glanced at Diego. He just frowned and went back to work. Indeed it seemed that what went on at Cuernavaca changed Maximilian. He appeared unshaven and spent less time working and more time on his horse or sleeping in his hammock. There were other rumors too. Rumors that he was being unfaithful to Charlotte. I couldn't be sure of these rumors. From his quarters there was a back door that led to the gardens. It would have been easy for anyone to leave or enter without being seen. I vowed that I should keep my nose out of his business, but Diego seemed more interested. "We must know what is going on." He said, "It will help when it's time to…" but wouldn't finish the sentence. "What?" I asked. "What will it help to know?" But he couldn't give me an answer.

We spent nearly two weeks in Cuernavaca, and when we returned to Chapultepec the castle was in an uproar. Some of the Belgians had been killed in an attack on their convoy: one of them a friend of the Empress. There was also new information from General Bazaine. He would be removing his troops in stages starting with the troops in the North. He would pull them closer and closer to Mexico City and Vera Cruz till finally only the troops in Mexico City would be left and they would return to France by way of Vera Cruz. "We have been betrayed," announced Charlotte, not even caring that the servants were nearby, "First by your brother and now by Napoleon." The mood around the city was that Maximilian would abdicate and return to Europe. Some of the servants disappeared and returned to their home villages. I began to wonder what I should do. Obviously I couldn't return to Europe by myself with no money. If the Emperor abdicated maybe I could return on his ship. Then I thought about my future in Europe. What could I do there? My skills were limited to laboring on the docks there. Here they were just about as limited. I went to bed that night confused.

The following week things became urgent for me as I was called in to His Majesty's office. "Her Majesty will be returning to Europe to seek help from Napoleon and the Holy Father. If you wish to return to Europe you may accompany her." I thanked him and returned to work. "What shall I do?" I asked Diego. "I like it here, but I won't have a chance like this to return again." He thought for a moment. "I don't think the Emperor will leave. He feels strongly that God has put him in this position and won't leave. You've told me about the Family Pact. He has nothing left there. He'll die here."

I thought about the offer for several days and finally told Diego. "I'm going to leave. I won't have another chance like this to get home and see family again." I left unsaid "like you," but Diego completed it for me. "Like me. You won't have this opportunity again. Go home."

The next few days were busy as we prepared for the Empress' departure. There were boxes to pack for her and all the serving ladies going to Europe.

On the morning of July 9, 1866 all was ready. I had my little pack that Georg had given me. It only had a few tokens that I had picked up over the years. The whole castle met together early as the sun was rising to say goodbye. Charlotte entered her carriage and Maximilian surprised everybody by joining her for the first part of the journey through downtown. They stopped at the outskirts of the city to say goodbye. Maximilian cried without shame and Charlotte looked like she was going to cry too. He finally pulled himself together as they said a final goodbye. I was driving one of the wagons but I had just enough time to give Diego a quick embrace before we departed.

The trip to Vera Cruz started out uneventful. We stopped at one village for the night and there were officials to greet Her Majesty and a reception following. Clearly the light of the Empire was bright here. The next day at Puebla it was different. Although there was a reception for Her Majesty, few people attended and local dignitaries sent their regrets. The Empress felt snubbed. The closer we got to Vera Cruz the worse it became. The Empress seemed depressed and not her normal self. One night close to midnight after everybody had gone to bed I was awakened by one of the ladies saying, "Her Majesty wishes to visit a friend in the country. Get the wagon ready." As I readied

the wagon I heard the ladies talk amongst themselves "I
tried to tell her it was too late but she wouldn't hear of it."
We arrived at a farmhouse in the country and the caretaker
was woken. "I'm sorry Your Majesty. They have gone to
Mexico City for safety." The caretaker told us. Charlotte
was left roaming the empty house by candlelight muttering
words we couldn't understand. The ladies finally
persuaded her to return to the inn where I was able to sleep
for an hour. The final night before Vera Cruz was the
worst. We arrived in one village and there was no
reception for Her Majesty. I was sent to an inn asking for
room for Her Majesty and entourage. There was enough
room but from inside I heard drunken singing:

Adiós Mamá Carlota
Adiós mi tierno amor
Se fueron los Franceses
Se va el emperador

Goodbye Mama Charlotte
Goodbye My Love
The French have left
The Emperor will go.

I went back and reported to the ladies in waiting what I
heard. Since there were no other options they told me to
get a room but not to tell who we were. I returned with
money to rent a room for the group. The Empress entered

as "Señora Gonzales" with her ladies to pass the night in a single room. I was left outside with the wagon and "Adios Mamá Carlota" going through my mind. I slept little that night thinking about the future and debating whether or not I should get on the ship.

The final day's journey went well and we arrived in Vera Cruz without problem. The Empress seemed distracted and not herself. She became upset though when she saw that the ship did not have a Mexican flag flying. "The Empress of Mexico will not enter a foreign ship." The captain had to search to find a Mexican flag and soon we were able to board. I debated dropping everything and staying in Mexico, but remembered Diego standing in the shop saying, "They're all gone," and realized I only had this chance to go back and make amends with my father.

ROME

I stepped aboard ship and in my mind said goodbye to one part of my life. I helped bring aboard the bags and valises of the elites who would be accompanying Charlotte in her attempt to persuade Napoleon not to pull his troops. I don't know what she expected the Holy Father to do. As I worked I thought about what I had learned in the last two years. I had, of course, learned Spanish. That was obvious. I had learned a lot about people and how to control my temper. Working two years for an Emperor who, no matter how nice he was, thought he was destined by God to rule had taught me that. I thought about the people whom I had encountered. The Countess, who had forced us to dance in the ball. She had left a life of luxury to come to Mexico and stayed longer than others. The French soldiers who had befriended Diego and I. They had helped us; had saved our lives and comforted us in Guanajuato. I had learned from them that soldiers could be caring, helpful men. Above all I had learned about Mexico and the many people who loved their country. Loved it enough to die for it.

"No." I surprised myself by saying out loud. "It's going to be difficult to go home." To my surprise, The Empress answered. "That's right, but we have responsibilities don't we?" She had been standing behind me on her way out to the deck. "Come. Let's wave goodbye to Mexico." She said. "We will see her again in just a few months." "You will." I thought. "I'll be staying in Rome."

The voyage proved rather comfortable. Since I wasn't listed as a stowaway this time I was assigned a berth in the sailors' quarters. It wasn't much more than a bunk in a room full of bunks but it was better than a mat on the floor that I had on the Navarre. Even better, I was not working all day and had some time to myself. The voyage reminded me of our voyage over. I was the only one allowed to bring food from the galley to Her Majesty's cabin. She seemed preoccupied when I delivered food to the cabin. I imagined she was worried about Maximilian, and by extension, Mexico.

As the ship got closer and closer to Europe I found myself doubting my decision to return home. What was I doing going back when I had changed so much in two years? I tried to imagine the first thing I would say to my father. I hoped he had forgiven me but I suppose I would understand if he hadn't. Then I wondered what I would do? I thought I had done a pretty good job for the Emperor of Mexico but I don't imagine that would translate to too many jobs in Rome. I don't think I could march up to the papal gate or Napoleon's door and say, "Excuse me. I used to be a bodyguard for the Emperor of Mexico and I'm pretty good driving wagons. Do you have a job for me?"

Fortunately or unfortunately my homecoming was put off for a few weeks as we docked in France first so the Empress could appeal to Napoleon right away. We landed at the port of Saint-Nazaire and nobody was at the dock to greet Her Majesty. I was sent onshore to see if there was a reception committee and found nothing. The ladies in waiting were angry at the lack of respect and finally I was sent to find transportation to the train station. It did not look promising to save the Empire. Her Majesty looked angry but said nothing.

Finally we made it to Paris and the Mexican embassy had made arrangements for a hotel. I was sent to the basement to sleep, but most of my time was spent waiting at the doors of the Mexican group to run errands or deliver notes. Her Majesty made two visits to Napoleon and returned after each visit looking less happy than before. After the second visit I was called to the room and she looked haggard and near tears. "Here. Take this to the telegraph office. Send it to His Majesty right away." Then she added, seemingly to herself, "All is lost. All is lost." I don't know what the Emperor Napoleon said but I understood from what I picked up from the ladies in waiting was that he had turned her down cold for more troops. It sounded like she had been turned out of the palace in tears but I wasn't sure. Charlotte was intent on finding help for Maximilian and so she ordered that we go to Rome. At least now I saw an end in sight for my stowaway journey. I helped gather all the bags to the train station and we were off to Rome. The journey took three days and when we finally arrived in Rome I was nervous with anticipation as was the Empress. As I arranged for transportation to the hotel I heard her tell a lady in waiting "I won't eat outside of the room. You must bring the food to me." I didn't think much about it at the time because I had brought food to her room for over two years now. We arrived at the hotel and I hardly had enough time to bring the bags up to the rooms that had been reserved when she called for me and said, "I don't want anyone else driving me. They are trying to kill the Emperor. You must drive me!" At this point I started to get a little worried about her. I could understand why she would only request me to drive as I had been her driver for two years now and she trusted me. I couldn't understand how she could think the drivers in Rome would be trying to kill the Emperor. Nevertheless, I simply bowed and said, "Yes Your Majesty."

So I was to be employed awhile longer it seemed. It gave me time to think about what to do or say to my father. The next day we went to the Vatican in a parade of coaches sent by the Vatican, but I was the only one she allowed to drive her carriage. As I pulled the carriage through the Vatican gates I remembered my thoughts on board the ship about knocking on the gates of the Vatican and I chuckled to myself "If Diego could see me now." I was directed to stop the carriage in front of the papal guards and as I helped her out of the carriage she was greeted by the representatives of the pope. Her Majesty left the carriage looking very happy and in control of herself. I was told to wait with the carriage and so I waited for the next two hours. When she finally returned with her ladies in waiting she looked depressed and not herself. Somewhere on the return to the hotel she suddenly shouted

"Stop! Get me a chicken! Get me a chicken!" I was shocked and started to say, "Your Majesty. I'm sure the restaurant at the hotel will have chicken prepared." She heard nothing and with a wild look in her eyes she shouted again, "Get me a chicken! Get me a chicken!" I stopped the carriage and looked at the lady in waiting with her. She simply said, "Yes Your Majesty. I will get a chicken, but let's get you back to the hotel first." We continued on to the hotel and I helped escort Her Majesty to her room. One of the ladies gave me a few coins and said, "Go to the market and get a chicken." And so I found myself looking for a market to purchase a chicken in a cage for the Empress of Mexico. When I returned about an hour later with the chicken I found them trying to feed the Empress but she would eat nothing. Looking at me she shouted "Prepare it! We shall cook it here. They are trying to poison me! They are trying to kill the Emperor!" I looked at the ladies in waiting who looked at me. I suddenly realized that I now had a new title of butcher to the Empress of Mexico.

I had never killed an animal before and it was not pleasant, but we were able to pluck the chicken and cook it over the fire in the room. I left as they served the Empress in search of water to clean myself. I went to the basement where I had laid out a mat to sleep on and wondered what was happening to the Empress. She had always been strong and used common sense. I remembered how I had heard a court official implying he would rather have her lead a meeting than the Emperor. I slept little that night and dreamed again of the Empress shouting "Bring me a chicken. Bring me a chicken."

The next morning I was called early before there was noise in the hotel or streets. "It's Her Majesty. She wants to take a drive." I was told. I quickly prepared a carriage from the hotel stables and met the Empress at the door. She again had a wild look and said, "Go. Go. Go." I didn't know where she wanted to go but took off on a tour around Rome. I decided that as long as I was driving I might as well try to see everything I could. Suddenly, in front of a fountain, she shouted. "Stop. Stop. Here! I must get water." She pulled a glass from her bag and jumped down from the carriage without help. "There! I can drink this water. They are trying to poison me!" She shouted again at the small crowd that had now gathered around the Empress of Mexico. "They are trying to poison me!" The ladies in waiting tried to coax her back into the carriage and from the crowd I heard people sighing and whispering amongst themselves. One person said, "That's Princess Charlotte of Belgium." Another said loud enough for all to hear. "She's Empress of Mexico. She's gone mad." I was able to pull away from the fountain with the Empress still holding the glass of water. Without being told I returned to the hotel. I felt at loose ends. I really wanted to leave here and be on my way back to home, but I also felt the need to protect the Empress whom I had protected for two years. I helped her out of the carriage and one of the ladies said as we escorted her to her room, "Here Your Majesty. Let's get you comfortable so you can sleep awhile." I spent the rest of the morning waiting to see what would happen. Sometime around noon I was sent to get another chicken. It was not any better the second time and I wondered if I should just leave and run home, but decided that I had signed up for the long term.

The Empress settled down some after the late lunch and I thought things would be ok. I was then surprised when she announced at twilight, "We will go now to the Vatican." The ladies in waiting tried to stop her saying that we hadn't been invited but Charlotte would hear nothing. "We are going to the Vatican now." She said firmly. I simply bowed my head and said, "Yes Your Majesty." I prepared the carriage like normal and the Empress was waiting as I pulled to the front of the hotel. When we arrived at the Vatican darkness had fallen and the gates were closed with guards standing in front. To my surprise she paid no attention to the guards and jumped out of the carriage and started pounding on the gates. "I must speak to the Holy Father! I must speak to the Holy Father!" She paused, as if for effect and shouted "Now!" By this time the guards looked worried and I noticed one of them had disappeared to a door at the side of one of the buildings. It didn't take too long and an official came out of the building and, taking one look at the Empress, ordered the gate open. From there I drove to the same spot I had driven the day before and waited. I waited for what seemed several hours, and hearing nothing from inside, I finally made a pillow out of my jacket and tried to sleep on the carriage seat. One of the guards leaving duty noticed me trying to sleep and went to his quarters and brought out a mat. I thankfully spread it out on the ground under the carriage and went sound asleep. When dawn came I was cold and miserable and knew nothing of what was happening inside. A guard came by with some food for me and said, "I think this is the first time a woman has spent the night in the Vatican." I stayed the whole morning at the carriage with only occasional breaks to relieve myself. Finally around noon the Empress appeared with a blank expression on her face and she looked lost. "We are leaving for Mexico today." She said in a sing song voice. I looked at one of the papal attendants and to one of the ladies. The papal attendant said, "Take Her Majesty back to the hotel and wait for instructions." I drove slowly back to the hotel and it seemed as if the whole of Rome was looking at the shrunken figure in the carriage. Later that afternoon a representative from the Vatican stopped at the hotel and soon I was called up to Her Majesty's room where she appeared to sit in a daze. "Here." I was told by one of the ladies who now seemed in charge. "Take this to the telegraph office immediately." I bowed and left the room but as I left I glanced at the address on the telegram. It was addressed to Charlotte's brother, the King of the Belgians. I delivered the telegram to the office and returned to the hotel to see if anything else was needed.

The woman who now seemed in charge thanked me and told me that would be all for the night. I returned to my basement home and was left wondering the fate of the Mexican Empire and the Empress who now seemed to have gone mad. I slept fitfully all night.

The next morning I awoke, and hearing no calls for service I finally went upstairs to wait outside Her Majesty's door. It wasn't till mid morning that the woman came out and said, "The King of the Belgians has sent word that he shall take responsibility for Her Majesty." She continued. "You are free to leave to find your family, however please leave your address so that we can reach you if necessary." I asked if I could say goodbye to Her Majesty and she said, "I think that would be very kind." I was ushered in to the room where Her Majesty was sitting at a desk. To my shock she took one look at me and shouted, "Traitor! Traitor! You are trying to poison me. You tried to kill the Emperor!" The ladies quickly tried to comfort her Majesty with, "It's Leo, Your Majesty. He's only come to say goodbye before he goes to his family. You remember him. He's been your driver and bodyguard and saved the Emperor's life once." She was not to be mollified and only screamed louder, "Traitor, Traitor." Before falling into tears at her desk. This had all happened so quickly that I didn't have time to think what was going on till I was pulled out of the room and led back to the hall. "Her Majesty has not been herself. I think it is time for you to go. Here is money for your pay and train fare leaving

Rome. Remember to leave an address where you can be reached." I thanked her and left. As I went to the basement to pick up my pack I checked the money she had given me. It was three times my usual pay plus more than enough for me to take the train to Civitavecchia. I stopped at the front desk on the way out the hotel and left the name of my father and his address in Civitavecchia to send to the Empress' suite. I left the hotel wondering if I would ever see them again.

HOME

I left the hotel happier than I thought I would for being newly unemployed. Having a pocket full of money helped. I was sad for the Empress. She had always been kind to me and I was sorry to see her reduced to a mind in torment. I thought about my future. I now had enough money to pay back Maria for what I had stolen and survive for several weeks. If I could stay at home and find work I would be able to save and make plans. I walked to the train station and discovered a train leaving for Civitavecchia almost immediately and purchased the ticket.

It was a three hour train ride to Civitavecchia and I used that time to rehearse what I was going to say. "Father. I'm sorry." Was the easiest, but it didn't seem like enough. "I'm sorry for all that I have done to you and could I please come home?" sounded self serving. "Is there anything I can do to make up for my past?" sounded too dismal. In the end I just quit thinking and looked at the scenery going by. In truth, I didn't recall taking this route before and everything looked new. The train pulled in to the station near the port and I pulled out my pack from above the seat and set out to find my family and face my past.

It was only a ten minute walk from the train station to the house, but it was starting to get dark by the time I turned up the street. I saw my father working outside the simple house and all thoughts about what to say left in a jumble of emotions as I ran to him crying "Daddy."

He looked up at me with a mixture of shock and surprise. When he realized it was me he enveloped me in a teary bear hug. "What… Where…How," were all the words he could say. Finally with another bear hug he released me while shouting, "Maria. Come. It's Leo." And it started all over again. After a few minutes I was pulled into the house and made to sit down. "Did you get my letters?" I asked. "Yes. Did you get our replies." It was then I realized that I'd never gotten any replies from them. As it turned out they had sent me several replies to my letters but none had made it through to Mexico City. I explained everything that had happened for the past two years. I told in detail how I had jumped aboard ship and hit my head and not come to till we were two days at sea. "I was just trying to run from the police. I didn't want to stowaway." I said. Father explained that the boys had been caught who pushed me in to robbing the Amici house. They had admitted that they had pushed me in to it and had paid for damages. "I don't think the police have any interest in you anymore." My father said. "Oh, here, I almost forgot." I said, giving Maria some money. "Here's to make up for what I took from you. I'm sorry. Please forgive me." With a laugh and a hug she refused the money. "That's long ago. The important thing is that you are home." We talked for hours as I told them all about the Mexican court and concluded with Her Majesty's sickness. "She didn't even recognize me and just called me a traitor. I felt terrible."

I realized that I hadn't asked about them. "What about you? Is everything ok?" They looked at each other. "Yes." Replied my father. "Everything is the same here. We just worried about you for a long time till we got your first letter. Then we were happy until lately when we've heard news about Mexico. They say that Napoleon will remove all French troops and leave Maximilian with only his Mexican soldiers." I explained everything I knew from what I saw, concluding with "I think when he finds out that Charlotte is sick and unable to get more troops from France he will come home." Maria nodded, and with empathy said, "Charlotte needs him if she is sick." And then, "Now it is time for bed. Come. Your room is ready." I went to sleep that night and felt at home.

I awoke the next morning with a start. I had slept on mats under carriages, basement floors and ships for so long I had to think where I was. When I remembered where I was I turned over with a smile and went back to sleep for a few minutes. When I woke again I went down to the kitchen where Maria was working. "Your father has gone to work at the docks. He says if you want to work go down and they will find something for you to do." We talked for a few minutes and before I left I said, "I want to apologize again for how I behaved to you. I have no excuse. You were trying to be a mother to me and I didn't respect that." She looked at me with love in her eyes. "That's all long ago and has been forgotten, but if you want me to forgive you I do so with all my heart." I left the house whistling as

I made the short walk to the docks. When I found my father he was at the same pier where it had all started: where the Navarre had been docked. "That's where it all started." I said, as I came up behind him. "I was able to jump the distance from the dock to the ship. This ship is just about the same size as the Navarre. I held on to a rope and shimmied up on deck. I think you would have been proud how I was able to climb." I concluded with a laugh. Father chuckled and said, "Come. Let's go to the harbor master's office and see if he has work for you to do." We walked to the office and I was introduced to the harbor master and we talked for a few minutes. "Well, right now I'll put you to work on repairing docks with the workers. If you can speak Spanish now I'll probably need you to translate the next time we get a ship from Mexico in."

My transition from royal bodyguard to day laborer was now complete. Instead of carrying a pistol I now carried a hammer. Instead of bowing and backing out of a room when talking to my employer I now just tipped my hat. The first afternoon when the supervisor had called us together to explain what had to be done I accidentally said, "Yes Your Majesty," and then felt embarrassed when everybody started laughing. I tried to explain where I had been working but the supervisor laughed it off. "I think I like it. I might start demanding it of everybody." When father and I walked home that evening it felt like a bond that had been broken was now whole. "Did you have a good day?" He asked. "I had the best day. I felt at home." I answered.

And so I developed a new normal of getting up early and spending the day on the docks working with my father and making new friends. News trickled out from Rome that His Majesty the King of the Belgians had taken responsibility for the Empress and she had been moved back to Belgium. Maria said a prayer for her and talked about the waste of a strong mind, taken down by illness. We talked about her and the Mexican situation for a couple of days and then, even that became old news as I settled in to life in Europe.

I was happy, or at least I told myself I was happy, but I longed for something else. I longed for adventure and travel. After two years of life on the ocean and traveling through Mexico I felt confined in the same job everyday. I never mentioned this to father or Maria, because I truly was happy to be home with them. I told myself that I was just having trouble adjusting to a new job and that the feeling would pass.

One day, two or three months after I had returned, I was working on the dock and I heard a shout. "Leo. Come here." It was the harbor master, and I thought maybe he needed me to translate for a recently arrived ship, but there had been no recent ships from Mexico. I arrived at the office, hat in hand, "Yes sir." The harbor master looked at me in amusement. "Well boy. You must be important. So important that the Mexican embassy sends you a telegram." I must have looked astounded because he laughed and said, "Yes, a telegram for you from the Mexican Embassy in Rome." I looked at the envelope and started to open it. Just at that moment my father walked in to say goodnight before going home. "What's that?" he asked. "A telegram from the Mexican Embassy for me," I said in amazement. "Well, what does it say?" I started to open it with trembling fingers. Inside all it said was "Come Embassy. Expenses paid. Important." I knew that telegrams cost money and that they were written to get the most information in the least amount of words. We stared at the telegram as if willing it to tell us more than it had. "I wonder what is so important that they sent a telegram instead of just a letter." My father answered simply. "Well. You won't know unless you go. Take the first train in the morning and find out."

The next morning I was up before dawn and, with a lunch Maria had made, I walked the short distance to the train station. Father walked with me and gave me a quick embrace before I left. "Don't let it be so long this time." He joked. "No, I promise." I said. "This time it won't be two years." I paid for the trip, being careful to get a receipt, for reimbursement. The three hour trip passed quickly and we pulled in to the train station at 9:00 AM. Since I had no pack I took off walking for the Mexican Embassy. When I arrived I showed the telegram at the door and asked who I should talk to. The guard at the door looked as if he were expecting me and quickly ushered me in to a reception room. I sat there for only a few minutes and was called in to another office where I was introduced to the Ambassador. "Well Leo." He said. "Have you missed your work for the Empire?" I replied truthfully that I was enjoying being home again, but I did miss the people of Mexico. "Well. I'm glad to hear that. I would like you to return to Mexico as my representative. We need important papers delivered to His Majesty as we can't trust telegrams anymore. The Americans deliver all telegrams to Juarez before they get to His Majesty." He paused as if waiting for me to agree immediately. "Well. What do you have to say?" I couldn't think for a moment, but I knew enough to ask "Why me? There are plenty of other people more important than I who could deliver a letter." He paused for a moment as if thinking of the best response. "Her Majesty is sick and we want him to know who is treating her. We also are not sure if His Majesty is in Mexico City, Chapultepec, or Queretaro. You are the only one we know who knows the best routes to all those places. Plus you are young and able to handle the ocean journey and the search for His Majesty. We have heard how you saved His Majesty's life." I stood there as if waiting for him to continue. He recognized that I wasn't going to agree too easily and said, "We, of course, will pay you and make sure that you have funds to return to Europe." I continued to stand there without saying anything. "Of course you will go as a diplomat. No more sleeping in basements or carriages. Her Majesty's ladies have told me what you did." I finally thought that I should say something, for in truth I was missing Mexico. "If I agree to go when should I leave?" I asked. "There is a ship leaving from here for Cuba and from there to Vera Cruz. We would need for you to be on the ship in six days. If you don't go we would send a letter by way of Vera Cruz and hope it makes it to His Majesty." Then he added. "If His Majesty abdicates you would return with him on the ship." Then he added, looking both ways, as if not wanting anybody to hear. "I'm sure that you will be returning in a matter of weeks."

I thanked him for the trust and said I would go home to talk with my father and return to tell him in plenty of time to get the papers and further instructions. "If I don't go I'll bring your letter to the ship to make sure it's posted by the captain once he gets to Vera Cruz." I offered. The Ambassador looked upset, but agreed. "I guess it's a lot to ask on short notice. If you could return the day after tomorrow with your response I wold appreciate it." Then in almost an afterthought, "Here is money for travel today and your return." handing me money without even asking for a receipt.

I walked back to the train station, even though, I suppose as nearly a diplomat, I could have called for a carriage. On the way back to Civitavecchia I thought of the pros and cons of leaving. On the pro side I had a chance to go back to Mexico, which I truly missed. I would have a chance to see Diego again, if he were still there. I would make more money than working on the docks. He had offered me that much. On the negative side I would have to leave my family again, but, I told myself, it would only be for a few months. If the Ambassador thought that His Majesty would return and declare the whole adventure over then he must have inside information. My thought was that he would not return ashamed of failure. I walked to the house nearly certain that I would take the offer.

To my surprise my father did not put up a fight. "It's your decision." He said. "You are young and will never have this opportunity again. If, as the Ambassador says, the Emperor will abdicate you would be home in a few months with money in your pocket and more stories." Maria looked troubled, but finally said, "The poor Empress. Maybe the papers you deliver will bring him back and help her recover." I went to work the next day and gave my notice. At the end of the day I told the Harbor Master. "I imagine I'll be back in a few months if you'll have me back." He smiled, "I think we'll find work for a diplomat."

Again I was up early to take the first train to Rome and arrived at the Embassy just as the Ambassador was arriving at the building. "Well. Have you come to a decision?" He asked. "I have sir. I would be glad to take the papers to His Majesty as a diplomat." He smiled. "Good. Let's prepare and get the documents ready." And he escorted me to his office. "The first thing I must tell you is that the Empress is very ill and under the care of a doctor. The letter to the Emperor tells more about her condition but that's all you need to know." He continued. "As a diplomat the documents we give you are not for other countries to ask for. If anyone asks you are to say that they are for His Majesty's eyes only." I asked "Are there many documents to be delivered?" I had visions of carrying trunks full of documents. He pulled out a small briefcase full of papers. "Not too many, but they are very important. We will lock the case and place the Imperial seal on it. You will not open it except in the presence of the Emperor." He looked at me. "Do you have clothing for the voyage?" I told him that I had only another change of clothes and "in Mexico I just wore what others didn't wear anymore." He took me to a secretary and said, "Make sure that he has some clothes to wear and a valise to carry." She took me to a storage room and started rummaging through boxes. "I think we have things that will work just fine for you." Suddenly I was reminded of the Countess as the secretary pulled out some trousers, shirts and jacket. "Here, try these on. Hurry. We don't have much time."

I left the storage room outfitted in new, to me, clothes and a valise packed with more clothes and enough money to buy passage on the ship to Mexico and travel to Mexico City or wherever I might find the Emperor. The Ambassador met me in his office saying, "Did you get enough clothes? And you have the money? Is it safe in your valise?" I assured him that I had more clothes than I had had in my life. He explained more about what was required of me. "You will land in Vera Cruz and make your way to Mexico City to find where the Emperor is. You will deliver the documents in your possession only to him. All you really need to know is that the Empress is sick and under the care of a doctor." I nodded in agreement. He continued "I have made the arrangements with the ship. They are expecting you onboard the day after tomorrow. You will have a cabin." He added with a smile. "No more sleeping in the galley, but you will not have the Imperial cabin." I laughed. "Anything will be better than sleeping in a stable like I've done." Then I added. "Much better than nearly being thrown overboard as a stowaway." He smiled. "Yes, I suppose so. Well. Let's get going. I have more to tell you and then we will take you to the station for the afternoon train to the port. I'll assume you can stay with your father for the next two nights?" "Yes sir, I'll make my goodbyes." He frowned, "The Empire rests in your hands" he said, I thought, somewhat melodramatically. I left the Embassy carrying two bags. One briefcase with the Imperial seal and one slightly larger suitcase with clothes and money hidden safely in a hidden interior pocket. I don't know which bag I was more worried about. The Ambassador called for a carriage and went with me to the train station. "Everything is arranged. Be safe and good luck."

I got to the train and sat in amazement. I would be traveling to Mexico as a diplomat. I couldn't believe this was happening to me. I sat for the three hour trip and marveled at my good luck. When I got home I showed father and Maria the clothes I had been given. I showed them the briefcase with the Imperial seal, but of course, I didn't open it. "When do you leave?" my father asked. "Day after tomorrow. The Ambassador said that he had made arrangements with the ship and I have a cabin. I don't have to stowaway!"

The next day was spent in putting the few things from home I needed in my case and walking to the dock and saying goodbye. When I got to the Harbor Master's office and told him what I was doing he said, "Oh. I knew. The ship came in this morning and I saw your name on the list of passengers leaving tomorrow." He continued. "It's a good ship. You should have no problems." That evening we had a little goodbye celebration. My father toasted, "To a safe journey for my diplomat son!"

The next morning I was up early to get to the ship since we would be leaving on the morning tide. My father and Maria accompanied me to the ship and I strongly embraced each of them before boarding. "I'll be back soon." I promised. "It won't be two years this time." With that I boarded the ship and said goodbye to Europe again. This time I was conscious as we sailed out of the harbor and I waved at my family till the dock was out of sight. At first I was excited to be on the ship as a passenger. I didn't have to work and I could spend the time doing whatever I wanted. I realized after a few days that I didn't have books to read or activities I could do besides walk the deck and talk to the other passengers. I knew I didn't have much in common with the other passengers, so I listened a lot at dinner and in the lounge. Finally, on the fourth day out, I gathered up my courage and introduced myself to one of the passengers after dinner. "Ah, good evening," came the reply. "I'm James Whitman. I'm on my way to Havana and from there I'll wait for Maximilian to leave or be killed in Mexico and then I will set up relations with the Juarez government to do business in Mexico." Of all the people on the ship to talk to I had picked an American supporting Juarez! I introduced myself, but left out any mention of the Empire or Maximilian. "Yes." He continued. "When that adventurer leaves Mexico will have a chance for a stable government and I want to be there to do business. So. What's taking you to Mexico?" I thought quickly. "Oh, I'm visiting friends I haven't seen for a while. I'll land in Vera Cruz and then try to find them in Mexico City." That much wasn't a lie. I would be looking for Diego and hoped he was in Mexico City. I thought it best to not mention that I was classified as a diplomat. "What is the prospect for business in Mexico?" I asked. "Well, it's not been good for Americans since our government hasn't had relations with Maximilian. How Napoleon ever thought he could put a monarchy in Mexico I don't know. They rebelled from Spain nearly 60 years ago. I think he was just hoping that the South would win the Civil War and the Confederacy would work with Mexico. Well, he didn't think that one through!" He said with finality. "Really," I said. "the North was sure to win the war?" "Oh yes." He said. "The North has all the industry and resources. What does the South have?" He asked. "Cotton." He said, answering his own question. "Cotton that Europe wants, but with the North blockading the ports there was no way for Europe to get the cotton. No. The South lost this war a long time ago and now there will be years to rebuild." Trying to get as much information as I could without telling him about my history I asked, "What will the Americans do now?" "Well," came the reply. "Volunteers will come across the border to help Juarez. Oh sure, some will come to help Maximilian, but Americans haven't had a king for 100 years and we don't want to see one next door. President Johnson isn't doing anything now, but he will. Mark my words. Johnson will not allow a monarch in his back yard. If Maximilian can't see that he's stupid. He needs to get out now or be killed. Well, very nice talking with you. I must meet my wife. I shall see you tomorrow." I thought about what he had said. I didn't think Maximilian was stupid, but after working for him for two years, I could see where Maximilian was idealistic and had the belief that God had ordained him to be Emperor. I also thought it pretty unlikely that he would leave Mexico. I wondered what was said in the letter I was delivering. If it told him that Charlotte was very sick he might leave. No. He is so used to the idea that God has ordained the Hapsburgs to rule that he would never leave. If Maximilian didn't leave I would have to work my way back to Europe or stay in Mexico. I decided that I would learn as much as I could from James to help me navigate what might be a rocky future.

The next day I received a note at breakfast inviting me to the Captain's table for dinner. I laughed when I saw the note. On board the Navarre when I was coming over the greatest honor one could receive was to be invited to dine with the Emperor and the second greatest honor onboard was to dine with the Captain. Here I was, a simple dock rat eating with the captain! I spent the day polishing my shoes and making sure that my one suit that had been pulled from the Embassy closet looked good. That evening I presented myself at the dining room with my invitation and was escorted to the Captain's table. The Captain greeted each person as we arrived and after I was introduced I looked around as the waiter introduced the next arrival, "Captain. I'd like to present James Whitman. Mr. Whitman. The Captain." The Captain smiled and greeted James. "Ah Mr. Whitman, pleasure to meet you. You've met Mr. Fiori the diplomat accredited to the Mexican Empire?" If I turned pale I hope nobody noticed it. I didn't think that the Captain would know about that. James looked a little surprised, but covered it well. "Yes, we've met." He said, shaking my hand. "Pleasure to see you again, but I think you have been keeping secrets from me." I thought quickly about how to answer in such a public place. "Oh we were having such a good chat I didn't see the need to burden you with stories about me." James smiled, "Oh I think I would like to hear stories. You must tell me sometime." The Captain invited everybody to the table and we were served a fine meal by waiters in white. I chuckled when I thought that was only a few months ago that I had been the waiter in white. After dinner James grabbed my elbow. "Come Leopold. Let's talk on the promenade deck where we can't be overheard. I have a feeling that you will need all the help you can get." I debated what I should tell James, but he seemed so open and honest I couldn't think of any reason to not tell him everything. I started with the fight with my father and being knocked out on the Navarre and ended with the meeting at the Mexican Embassy. "And so I'm here to deliver papers to His Majesty." I concluded. James had listened carefully to everything with only a nod or a "hmm" to add. "Well, you have led an exciting life the last couple years, but have you considered the reason they asked you to deliver the letter is that nobody there wanted to travel to a war zone and give up the comforts of Europe?" I told him that I had but also what the Ambassador said that he was pretty sure that Maximilian would abdicate and I could come home with him. "But in your heart you believe that Maximilian would never willingly give up the throne?" James asked. "I believe there's a good chance he would want to remain." I answered. "He believes strongly that God has anointed him to be Emperor." "Yes. Yes. Yes. The Divine Right of kings," interrupted James. "Something said for 1000 years to justify stomping a person to the ground when they don't know their place" I laughed. James had a funny accent but I liked his openness and humor. I wondered if all Americans were like him. He continued. "I think that the Embassy is using you but you need to complete your assignment. Listen. We will meet everyday so I can tell you what's been happening in Mexico and the world and then we will plan your actions once you land in Vera Cruz. You'll need to watch your back."

For the remainder of the voyage we met daily to talk about the situation in Mexico, Europe and the United States. I grew to enjoy our talks and he started teaching me English. "I suppose I'm teaching you American." He said after one of our lessons. "The British have a different accent than we do. I don't think they would even admit that we speak English." He joked. "Have you lived there?" I asked. "Oh yes. I studied and worked in London before heading to France. That's where I decided that there might be some opportunities for business in Mexico when Maximilian leaves." I asked why there would be opportunities. "The French will be gone. The Americans are next door and ready to do business after the Civil War. I see no reason why Juarez wouldn't be willing to overlook our past history and do business with us." I pondered this for a moment, "You mean that he would be willing to make money?" James howled. "Exactly! When there's money to be made any politician is willing to work with just about anybody. But now we need to start thinking about you and how you're going to get to Mexico City and beyond. Have you thought about that?" I told him that I thought I could make it easily between Puebla and Mexico City and from there to Queretaro or Cuernavaca or wherever His Majesty might be in Central Mexico. "I know enough people between Puebla and Queretaro from working for His Majesty that I can pass the night anywhere. I've slept in plenty of stables over the last two years." I concluded with a laugh. James laughed too. "We won't worry about that then. But how will you get from Vera Cruz to Puebla? Those areas aren't safe for the Empire."

Getting closer to Vera Cruz my anxiety began to deepen. I hadn't been in Mexico for several months and I really had no idea of what had happened. The news that I had heard didn't make it sound good and with the French gone I was sure that it might be dangerous. I needed to start thinking about how to find Maximilian. Vera Cruz had always been supportive of the Empire so I knew I was safe there. From Vera Cruz to Puebla could be difficult, and this time I wouldn't have the safety of an army convoy. I asked James if he had any experience traveling solo in dangerous places. "Well, I could make up stories about escaping Indians or being in the middle of a battle between the French and Austrians, but no, I've never led that exciting a life. My best suggestion is to make yourself look normal so nobody pays attention to you." He looked at me. "The clothes that you got from the Embassy make you look too rich. I know they were hand me down clothes from some rich person but I think they'll look out of place trying to get from Vera Cruz to Puebla. Wear your old clothes that you've worn for a couple years now." Taking a good look at me. "And the sealed bag that they gave you to deliver: hide it. Put it in your other bag underneath clothes. We don't want anybody to see it and think that you are an easy mark for theft." I agreed that those were all good ideas. "I think I can take the train as far as it goes from Vera Cruz without problems and then go with a convoy from one of the villages to Puebla. It will take a few nights but it should be fairly safe." James smiled. "Good. Listen. Here is my card with my American address and French address. If you get in trouble in Mexico ask around in Mexico City or Queretaro for me. I might not be there but many of the non French business people know my name and if they can't get in touch with me they might be able to help you." I thanked James profusely and asked "How long will you remain in Cuba?" "Only as long as necessary. I can't do much business in Cuba. The Spaniards have made sure of that. They'll control all business. I need to wait just long enough for Maximilian to be gone or out of the picture to set up deals with Juarez forces. I'll probably be behind you a few weeks." Since that night was the last night before we arrived in Cuba I carefully put his card in my bag with my money. I hoped I wouldn't have to use too much of that money to get to

Mexico City and I hoped that if I did find Maximilian that he would give me enough to get back to Rome. Then I thought, "What if I don't go back to Rome? What if I decide to stay?" I put the thought out of my mind as I saw the lights of Havana at night.

The next morning James greeted me at the gangplank. "OK. All set! Good luck to you! Remember if you need something ask around. I'm off!" and he walked down the gangplank. We were just going to spend a few hours in Havana to pick up passengers and some supplies before we headed to Vera Cruz so I didn't even bother to leave the ship. By late afternoon I could hear the ship's whistle and I knew we were on our way.

It took several days to travel from Havana to Vera Cruz. We passed by the northern point of the Yucatan and I remembered that the Empress had traveled there without Maximilian and had been treated so well by the Indians. I wondered again how she was doing and thought about the last time I saw her when she accused me of trying to poison her. I didn't pray often, but when I thought of her, I said a quick prayer. Then, as long as I was praying, I prayed that I could get through to the Emperor.

On the sixth day out of Havana I could see the lights of Vera Cruz and I started to pack my few belongings with the Imperial case at the bottom of my case with clothes on top. We docked late at night so I stayed onboard till first light and then I ventured out on to Mexican soil for the second time in months. I walked around the dock area and found that it hadn't changed much in the few months I'd been gone, or even in the two years since I first came here. I walked to the train station and asked when the next train would go up the mountains toward Puebla. I bought a ticket for Cotaxtla which would get me there in a few hours. From there I would have to take a coach or walk to Cordoba and Puebla. But first I would need to find out where His Majesty was. I knew that Vera Cruz was safe in the Empire's hands so I felt safe in asking anybody what was happening. I came upon a man selling newspapers, and, giving him a coin, asked for the news about Maximilian. "He's going to stay I think." The newspaper man said. "People were trying to get him to abdicate, but I think he's waiting to hear news from the Empress before he decides. I don't think she has sent him news about help from Europe." He concluded. I didn't enlighten him about Charlotte's condition, but asked if he knew where he was now. "Back in Mexico City. He won't live in the palace, and Chapultepec has been torn apart by looters so he's staying in a small place in Mexico City." I couldn't believe that looters had destroyed Chapultepec. It had been his prize and he loved living there. "None of the rich haciendoros want him so he lives like a peon. Tough times ahead for this country." He concluded. I thanked him and walked back to the train station to wait for the train. Things didn't look good for Maximilian and I wondered if the letter I was delivering would help him make up his mind once and for all.

To save money I had purchased a second class ticket. I wanted to save as much money as possible in case I was forced to live here for awhile. My money was still safe inside my bag and I was careful to only take out money when nobody was looking. As the train left the station I wondered how I would go on to Puebla. I supposed I would look for a caravan heading out of Cotaxtla once I got there, but till then I could only sit and wait.

The train ride only lasted a few hours but it was growing dark as we pulled in to Cotaxtla and I knew that I would be spending the night here before venturing on. I found the inn where the elite had stayed when we came through two years ago but knew I couldn't afford it, or didn't want to afford it. I saw a man working by a house and stable and asked if I could sleep in his stable tonight. He looked at me a little surprised. "I'm sorry sir. I just arrived and will be on the way tomorrow and can't spend a lot of money on a hotel. I've spent many nights on a stable floor. It doesn't bother me." A smile spread across his face. "Well, if you're willing to sleep in a stable I think you're safe enough to have in the house. Come in." He introduced himself as Jorge and took me in to meet his wife who promptly put some food on a plate in front of me. "Come, sit down and have something to eat. You don't want to eat at any inn. They don't have food like this." As we ate I questioned them about the country. "Yes, Maximilian needs to leave. We don't need foreigners here. Mexicans need to be in charge of their own destiny." Jorge said. His wife added, "I remember when Carlota passed by here a few months ago. Oh they were singing 'Adios Mama Carlota' and jeering at her. I felt sorry for her, but she and the Archduke shouldn't have come." I smiled at His Majesty being called 'The Archduke.' I was so used to calling him 'sire' or Your Majesty' that I had forgotten he was a prince of Austria. She mistook my smile for laughing at the song. "Yes. It's a funny song. Sometimes I catch myself singing it." She said with a laugh and started singing

Adiós Mamá Carlota
Adiós mi tierno amor
Se fueron los Franceses
Se va el emperador

We all laughed and I thanked them for the dinner and asked if I could sleep in the stable. Jorge brought me to a small room and said, "This is better than the stable, but not much. Tomorrow we will work on finding you a way to Puebla."

I slept well that night on the bed that they had made up for me. I dreamt of Charlotte singing 'Adios Mama Carlota' while Maximilian was standing in the background saying ,"Don't leave me Charlotte." The morning sun woke me and I shared a quick breakfast with Jorge and we walked down the street to ask about a caravan. "Yes," shouted a man. "We're leaving in 20 minutes. We need another wagon driver. Can you drive?" I answered truthfully. "Yes, I've driven wagons and carriages. I can shoot pretty good too, but right now I don't have a weapon." I didn't find it necessary to say where I had learned to drive or fire weapons. I quick said goodbye to Jorge and threw my bag in the wagon that the wagon master pointed out. It looked like I wouldn't have to pay for this trip either.

THE SEARCH FOR HIS MAJESTY

The trip was uneventful the first day and I enjoyed the time driving. We slept that night under the stars near an Indian village. The next morning we were on our way early in hopes that we could make it to Puebla in two more days.

Pulling in to Puebla I noticed that the banners that had been flying for Her Majesty were all gone and some posters for the Emperor had been defaced. I walked around the city trying to get an idea of where the city stood politically. I finally decided that it would be safe to ask if anybody knew where the Emperor might be and tried the same tactic with a newspaper man. "Oh. He's gone. He was here, but he's back in Mexico City now I'm sure." That was twice I had been told he was in Mexico City so I set out looking for transportation there and found another caravan heading toward Mexico City and the train station.

I walked the final distance from the train station to the National Palace. I hoped that some of the people at the National Palace would remember me and give me an idea where Maximilian was. I was in luck. One of the guards at the door remembered me and allowed me inside. "So. Where have you been? I haven't seen you in a long time," he asked. I explained that I had gone to Europe with Charlotte but now was back. "You came back! Things are bad here. His Majesty looks sick and the rebels are getting closer." He finished by telling me where the Emperor was staying and "Welcome back to Mexico. I hope you won't be sorry."

I walked the streets of Mexico City looking for the house where the Emperor was staying. When I found it I was surprised that the man who always insisted on things being perfect could stay in such a poor place. I knocked on the door and to my surprise Eloin answered. "Leo! You've come back! Come in. Do you carry word from Her Majesty and Europe?" I answered in the affirmative and that I had a letter for His Majesty that I was told to deliver only to him. "Well then, I suppose you won't let me look at it. Come in and I shall tell his Majesty." A voice came from the other room. "That's not necessary, welcome home Leo." I bowed,"Your Majesty. I bring you a letter from the Mexican Ambassador to Rome." Pulling the briefcase with the imperial seal out of my bag I handed it to him. "Thank you. I'm glad they sent you." While His Majesty was reading the letter I studied his face. He did look sick. Much sicker than he had ever looked before. He looked at me. "Did the Ambassador tell you what was in the letter?" "No Your Majesty." He continued speaking to Eloin "Who is this Doctor Smith treating Her Majesty?" Eloin answered "He is a Psychiatrist from Vienna. Why?" The Emperor looked upset "Were you with the Empress when she turned ill?" I felt bad having to tell what I had seen and how she had insisted on going to the Vatican late at night and calling me a traitor. "Oh my poor Charlotte." Maximilian muttered under his breath. Then "Look at this

Eloin!" He shouted "'Will not be allowed to return to Austria.' Look what my brother says. He means to humiliate me even more. I can't go back to Austria as Emperor of Mexico or heir to Austria. This settles it. I can't go back. I must stay here and fight! We shall head to Queretaro and put up our fight."

QUERETARO

I think the Emperor had already decided to stay, but the letter confirmed that he had little left in Europe with Charlotte ill and his brother unwilling to accept him as heir or Emperor in Austria. I decided that France and Austria and most of the other countries of Europe had given up on Mexico and my best hope for returning to Europe was with Maximilian in exile or as a paying passenger on a ship for which I couldn't afford. For now I was stuck with Maximilian going to Queretaro. I was sent back to the palace for the night with instructions to tell the guard to be ready to leave at a moment's notice. "Yes, we will be ready." The guard told me. "Although with the French gone there are not too many soldiers here to go to battle against the rebels." He went on to explain that as the French left many soldiers had taken it as an opportunity to defect also. Some heading to the rebel side and some just leaving to try and make it home before war came to them. We finished talking about the Emperor and I asked if he had seen Diego. "Not for a long time. I don't think he's working for the Emperor anymore. It's hard to say. The city is in chaos and the Emperor hasn't stayed in one place too long. He's traveled from Cuernavaca to Puebla and all places in between. No wonder people came in and looted the castle at Chapultepec. Nobody's been there to safeguard it. Diego could be working for the Emperor elsewhere or he just left. I hope you find him."

The next few days were spent gathering together whatever soldiers were left in Mexico City and on the morning of February 13, 1867 we left with the Emperor leading the army, as poor as it was. The three day trip to Queretaro was uneventful. Considering there were rebels everywhere I was surprised that we did not face any opposition. One of the soldiers told me that Juarez was working his way south from near the American border and that it seemed that Queretaro would be where the two forces would meet. "The Emperor has his generals in the field and they are both heading toward Queretaro." I was told. I myself, didn't want to be heading toward a war zone, but it seemed that Maximilian was my ticket back to Europe. Part of me was also hoping to find Diego again.

On the afternoon of the third day we arrived in Queretaro and set up camp in the middle of town. It didn't really seem like a war zone. Some of the rich people of town had made room for Maximilian and his entourage in their homes. I was again left to fend for myself, but after two years I was pretty good about getting shelter in a stable somewhere. It was on one of those days when I was heading back to the stable after spending the day running errands for His Majesty that I saw in the distance a person who looked like Diego. I ran for the corner where I saw him turn and shouted "Diego." He looked up and a huge grin broke across his face. "Leo! You came back!" We embraced in a huge bear hug and then, "You shouldn't have come back. It's not safe! But I'm glad you did." He asked me where I was staying, and said he had a room in a house not far from the center of town. "Here, bring your stuff and stay with me. We can set up a mat on the floor. It's better than a stable." I agreed and we took my bag out from where I hid it during the day. I had carefully kept my money in a bag around my neck hidden under my shirt. "Why did you leave Mexico City?" I asked, although I had an idea that he was not happy working for the Emperor. He paused and looked at me. "You know after I found out how my family was killed I couldn't work for him anymore." Then, looking at me with indecision in his eyes, "If I tell you something will you promise to keep it to yourself and not tell the Emperor or army?" I had an idea what he was going to say and in my heart of hearts I knew he was right. "I promise." I said. "We are friends." Diego looked at me. "No. We are brothers. That's why I can tell you. I've been working for the rebels. Oh. I'm not a soldier. I don't think I could kill a man, but I left Mexico City not long after you left. It wasn't the same without you and all I could think of was that I was working for the man who had killed my family. I knew that I had to get out. I planned it carefully and saved as much money as I could. Then I decided that I could do good by providing information to the rebels." I laughed. "Oh. You are a spy!" He darkened. "Shh. I haven't told you everything." Then, looking both ways as if checking for spies, he continued. "Yes. I suppose you could say I'm a spy, but you must be quiet. Things have changed since you left." I apologized.

"I'm sorry. You're right. I haven't been here. What's changed?" Diego looked at me. "Maybe you haven't heard. The Emperor signed a decree saying that anybody who takes up arms against the Empire now loses any right of appeal and the army can execute any rebel without worrying about reprisal. Remember when Maximilian pardoned the man who tried to kill him?" "Yes." I said. "I remember that the soldiers were upset that he was let go. Wasn't Maximilian trying to show mercy?" "Right." Diego said. "But remember when he caught us and tried to kill us? The soldiers came and rescued us and took the man out and shot him. They didn't tell the Emperor what had happened. Remember? Lopez just said, 'Oh some target practice.' They executed him because they didn't want the Emperor to pardon him again." I was puzzled. "What does that have to do with the Emperor signing a decree?" Patiently Diego said, "See. Everything is coming to a head. The army has finally made Maximilian become hard." "So how does this work with you giving information to the rebels?" I asked. "I listened as much as I could whenever I drove or helped in the house. When I heard the Emperor agree to sign the decree I knew that I needed to help Mexico. I can't be a very good soldier, but I can provide information. I found a person who sympathized with the rebels and asked how I could help. He had me stay in Mexico City gathering information and then sent me here to be his ears. I've been feeding information to the rebels by way of him." He concluded the story. "Wow!" I exclaimed, and then, without thinking, "Who did you ask?" Diego frowned. "You know you're my brother, but I can't tell you that. I shouldn't have told you this much. Remember. You promised." I realized my error. "I know. I'm sorry. Just tell me what you want. I won't ask anymore questions. Diego smiled. "Good! I won't tell you anymore now. You tell me about you!" I told him the whole story about Charlotte and meeting my family again. "I'm glad you persuaded me to leave. I came back on good terms with everybody." Diego smiled. "I figured that your family would take you back. That doesn't surprise me." We continued talking far in to the night till we both fell asleep.

Over the next several weeks things began to happen on the battle front. There were skirmishes outside of town as rebels came closer to the city and the army went out to take them on. I continued to stay with Diego in the room near the center. Barricades had been set up to define what the Empire considered 'safe' territory. Our house was just inside the safe zone. I spent my days running errands and Diego did too. He never told me where he went or who he talked too. He seemed to know what the Emperor was doing and sometimes slipped out of the barricades in the morning after we got out of bed and was gone all day, returning late at night when I was just getting in to go to bed. "Be careful now." He said one night. "The end is coming. The battles will start tomorrow. We need to move away from here. The Emperor will be at the convent, and we need to be there where it's a little safer." I stood looking at him amazed. "How did you know that the Emperor had moved there? He just did it today." Diego frowned. "Never mind. Get your stuff together. We need to get out of here. This building won't be safe. It's too close to the barricades. We will be killed if we stay here." We got our few possessions together and left the house that had been our home for a couple months. "We can stay in a stable again. We've done that before!" Diego said with a smile. We got our bags hidden in the second level of the stables where they kept food. I was ready to bed down, but Diego said, "I have to go for a few minutes to talk to somebody. I'll be back." And with that he was gone. He had my curiosity and so I followed him as best I could. He left the convent area and down a side street till he met a man and they talked for a few minutes. I got as close as I could till I realized that Diego's informant was Lieutenant Lopez! One of the Emperor's trusted aides was helping the rebels! I turned and ran back to the stable so I could look asleep when Diego came back. I pretended to be asleep when he got back. He lay down next to me on his mat and whispered. "Remember. You promised." I lay there and said. "I know. I won't say a word." I didn't sleep much that night and could only think about our relationship and what I had been through the last two years. Finally, in the morning, I looked at Diego. "I'm ready to help. What do I do?"

HILL OF THE BELLS

Diego looked at me. "Right now just what you've been doing. We need to stay safe right now." As if to remind us of our situation the sounds of war started with cannon fire.

The day seemed to go on forever. Cannon and rifle fire echoed through the town. Maximilian was seen at the barricades talking to soldiers and trying to encourage them in the battle. Diego was here and there too. He seemed to disappear on one side of the barricades and reappear later on the other. Finally in the evening the sounds of war settled down and it seemed a strange quiet settled over the city. Diego appeared behind me. "I need your help now. You can get close to the emperor. Go find where everybody is and give this note to Lopez. Don't tell anybody and don't let yourself be seen." I took the note and realized that I had just turned traitor. I worked my way back to the convent. The Emperor had just returned. "Well Leo. Thank you for your help. You've been invaluable the last two years. Maybe we will have peace now." "Yes Your Majesty, I hope so too. Good night," I replied. I left as quickly as I could in search of Lopez. I saw him walking toward the room the Emperor had just entered. I sidled up to him and quietly put the note in his hand as I walked by and disappeared in the darkness. I ran back to the stable and told Diego. "Good. We'll watch now." Pretty soon we saw Lopez leave on his stallion heading toward the barricades. I started to ask "What's going on…," but was shushed with a quick "Watch." Soon Lopez was back and another person came from the shadows running toward the main part of the convent where Maximilian was staying "Quick." He shouted. "We have been betrayed! Save the Emperor!" A commotion commenced in the convent and soon the Emperor came out with some of his aides. "Quick," whispered Diego. "We'll follow." We followed at a safe distance and as we approached the barricade where soldiers should have been there was nobody. "We'll try to escape from here," we heard the Emperor, but it was too late. From the shadows rode a rebel general surrounded by mounted soldiers. Maximilian I, Emperor of Mexico, looked up and said, "Well. It would appear that I have been captured," and gave up his sword to end the Empire.

From then everything seemed to speed up and slow down at the same time. Maximilian was taken away by the now victorious rebels. Diego pulled me away. "We need to get away now. Let's get our stuff. We will go where it's safe." Grabbing me by the arm he led me through the city. "Soldiers will be deserting now. The Empire is dead and you need to be seen on the winning side. I think we are safe but we need to get away from here. Thank you for delivering the note. I couldn't have gotten so close." I wondered if I had just brought down the Empire.

The next few days were stressful. We watched as rebels streamed in to the city and Imperial soldiers fled leaving uniforms behind. Soon Juarez entered the city and set up headquarters. Diego and I were able to see people come and go to see him and then we moved back to the convent where Maximilian was held prisoner and saw people come to see him. The guards seemed to let him have visitors without problem. Once I was outside the convent and one of the aides came to me. "Here. Take this to the Emperor," and handed me a note. I was a little afraid, but went to the guard and told him I had a note "For the Archduke" and was granted entrance. Maximilian looked up when I entered his cell. "Well Leo. It looks like you have it better than I do now." He joked. "What have you?" He took the note and read it. "Well. They want me to escape, but they say nothing about the others. I don't think I can do that. We are destined by God to rule and sometimes this is what happens." Thank you for coming. Give my greetings to everybody."

We listened to the reports that were coming in from around the world. It seemed that everybody was asking Juarez for Maximilian to be freed. Juarez was holding firm and was heard to say. "All Mexico calls for a trial." Soon there was a trial of Mexican officers who, taking into account the decree that Maximilian had signed, sentenced him to death. Again there were telegrams from around the world asking for pardon. Most people were under the impression that if Maximillian were pardoned he would just go back to Europe and try to lead a rebellion from there. I think that he would have gone back to Austria and never been heard from again, but that was not my decision.

One day in June all the appeals were over. Maximilian was taken from his convent cell early one morning and brought out to the "Hill of the Bells," where he was executed with his generals. The empire was over.

After some discussion Diego and I left Queretaro. He had nothing in Guanajuato anymore, but cousins in Vera Cruz. I, of course, had no family in Mexico, and although James Whitman had promised help he wasn't in Queretaro. Juarez wouldn't release Maximillian's body and I was hoping I could go home if they ever released it. "You might as well come with me. The Juarez government won't ask you to accompany a body to Europe." Diego said. "We can work our way to Vera Cruz and maybe you can work as a deckhand to Europe. " I don't know if I will ever get home, but I do know that I am with friends.

25697363R00104

Made in the USA
San Bernardino, CA
13 February 2019